LAST RIGHTS

LAST RIGHTS

A Novel

Charles Deemer

Round Bend Press
Portland, Oregon
2018

Round Bend Press
1115 SW 11th Ave.
Portland, OR 97205

Printed in the USA
ISBN 978-0-9965266-5-4

Cover photography from Creative Commons.
Back cover drawing by Thomas Strah.

roundbendpress@yahoo.com
roundbendpress.blogspot.com

Acknowledgments

Several readers offered valuable feedback on the first presentable draft of my manuscript: Rev. Dr. Marilyn Sewell, Tom Strah, Lynne Fuqua and my wife Harriet Levi. The novel is better for their suggestions and probably worse for the suggestions I ignored.

Dedication

To the memory
of my brother
Bill Deemer
1945-2018
the Poet of the family

IN A ZEN MANNER

No more apologies for existing.
No more demands to change your behavior.
I'm incorrigible, you're a hopeless case.
The sun shines on both of us anyway.

*

No one sick with loathing towards me.
No one miserably in love with me.
Friendly towards all, friends with none.
Head in the clouds, feet on the ground.

The character CJ first appears in my novel *Sodom, Gomorrah & Jones*, to which this can be considered a sequel. However, *Last Rights* also stands on its own.

CD
8/10/2018

I am dying from the treatment of too many physicians.
Alexander the Great

The art of living well and the art of dying well are one.
Epicurus

Life must be a constant education; one must learn everything,
from speaking to dying.
Gustave Flaubert

PART ONE

I grow old ... I grow old ...
I shall wear the bottoms of my trousers rolled.
T. S. Eliot

Who's Who in Academia?

Carlton James ("CJ") Jones Professor Emeritus (retired), Department of History, Portland State University.

Retired 2004.

Author, *From Where the Sun Now Stands*; *Settling the West: A Short History; Forked Tongue: Andrew Jackson's Indian Policy; The American Indian Question: Assimilation or Genocide?*

Ph.D., History, University of Oregon, 1964.

Teaching career: University of Wisconsin, 1964-6; University of Montana, 1966-70; University of Oregon, 1970-2; Portland State University, 1972-2004.

Member of American Historical Association, Western History Association, Native American Heritage Association, World Folk Music Association.

1

No one, thought CJ, would see it coming. Molly, who apparently was in love with him, would take it especially hard. A few former colleagues at Portland State University might talk about it after the fact, looking for clues in memory that such a thing might happen. Joe Smart, another historian and CJ's frequent road companion in recent years, would be bombarded with questions. Had he or his wife Jan seen it coming?

CJ could well imagine that Jan Smart would have a theory. She had a theory about everything, especially after the fact. She would say yes, she had seen this coming, that the ascension of Donald Trump had greatly depressed CJ and driven him to such extremes. She'd throw in a quotation or two from Shakespeare, her academic focus – "to be or not to be" came to mind – and turn him into a tragic hero. No, an existential hero! She would recite her theory with considerable energy and confidence but she would be wrong.

In fact, no one would come close to CJ's motivation because no one would look for an explanation so simple, so uncomplicated, so rational, so divorced from the usual motivators of depression or guilt or personal crisis. His best friend Matt might be the exception and understand what CJ was really doing, but he'd also turn the idea into a joke. CJ could hear his friend telling him, *How can you leave this world when the young women get more beautiful and uninhibited every year?*

CJ had reached his decision because he was determined to manage his own death. He had gone through Helen's ordeal with cancer, a long dance of hope and horror managed by her doctors, and he had seen her life prolonged by a sequence of treatments at the expense of comfort and quality of living. She was alive, yes, but much of the time she also was miserable. He was determined to avoid the same dance at the end of his own life. He would choose comfort over longevity.

Presently CJ felt fine, at least for an 81 year old man with arthritis, a bad back and a cynical disposition, with the misfortune of being a citizen in Donald Trump's United States. To be sure, he felt worse as he got older, year by year, and lately suffered frequent stomach cramps, but at the same time he felt blessed to be as old as he was for two reasons: he had lived most of his life in a time when media did not constantly bombard one about the state of the world, which almost always featured bad news and never more so than in the present era of Trump; and with luck he would be dead of natural causes before the worst of the climate crisis – the food and water riots, the millions of desperate refugees roaming the planet, the continued global disruption and decay of democracy – made life unbearable everywhere.

Jan Smart was right about one thing: the ascension of Trump had troubled him and compromised CJ's efforts to drop out of citizenship. This had been a primary motivation in leaving Portland, abandoning his apartment to live in a van on the road. He had been a news junky most of his adult life but even before Trump the daily avalanche of news had become so stressful, so upsetting, so unrelenting, that he vowed to stop paying attention to it. He was "dropping out," to use a phrase from the sixties. He thought of this as resigning from citizenship. He would just "live" his life, in the manner of Thoreau, and forget about making the world a better place.

And this new attitude had worked reasonably well, despite his checking the news on television whenever he got a motel to clean up. On the road he found a new appreciation for Nature and began a photo blog of the landscapes he found on his travels. Soon CJ had a routine that was relaxing and mellow. The world could go to hell, he was living his final years in relative peace.

And then Donald Trump ran for president. And won.

How could CJ ignore the fact that a thin-skinned, ignorant, sexist, racist moron was in control of the world's largest nuclear arsenal? How could he ignore that the President of the United States thought climate change was a Chinese hoax? Trump brought worry and stress back into CJ's life. The mere sound of Trump's voice, his photo on a newspaper page, a flash of the man on TV, could induce feelings of nausea. And Trump's tweets, which were endlessly repeated in the media, could send CJ into a rage. What had happened to intelligence? What had happened to civility?

But not only Trump: his supporters upset CJ more than the man himself. Trump, after all, was not the first politician to sling mud and play dirty politics. He might insinuate that

Obama was Muslim but supporters of John Quincy Adams had accused rival Andrew Jackson of cannibalism, feeding on Indians he had massacred. Grover Cleveland was accused of siring an illegitimate child. Hamilton accused Jefferson of having an affair with one of his slaves, which turned out, according to many historians, to be true. In one of history's great ironies, LBJ defeated Goldwater by convincing voters the senator was a warmonger and LBJ the peace candidate. CJ knew the historical record, and Trump's behavior was far too common.

Yet Trump was different in one respect: his deceptions and shortcomings were self-evident without effort to disguise them. There was no question Trump was a liar because he bragged about it; no question he was a cheater because he bragged about it; no question he was a sexist because he bragged about it. And yet his supporters stuck by him. Indeed, as Trump himself had bragged once again, he could shoot someone on the streets of New York and not lose a vote.

Who were these loyal mindless enthusiasts? There were millions of them and they defined an America that CJ, for all his lifelong criticism of American policies, no longer recognized. A man's character no longer mattered. Facts no longer mattered. The Earth was flat, science was a scam, and you could believe anything that occurred to you because truth didn't exist. American politics had become Donald Trump's personal Reality TV Show, which for CJ presented a nightmare of increasing distress.

CJ believed Trump, and his many supporters, represented a victory of ignorance and bigotry, the last gasp of a dying oligarchy, white, male. Was the victory a brief fluke or a new age in our evolving history? CJ knew one thing: Nature didn't care one way or the other. It was probably too late for politics to influence climate change.

So the question CJ began asking himself was, Why stick around for the inevitable decline and disaster? If he waited too long, a stroke could destroy his ability to control his own destiny. Living, in other words, had become a daily risk to his own empowerment, and the risk was greater the older he got. Hence the consideration of taking matters into his own hands, of managing his own death sooner rather than later.

The more CJ thought about this, the angrier he got because he lived in a culture where death was managed by religion and by the medical profession, neither of which would take his concerns sympathetically. A physically healthy old man taking his own life was considered a tragic act of mental imbalance.

In contrast, CJ began to think of his own suicide as an act of gratitude (for a long, blessed life) and empowerment (he was still physically and mentally functional). In a culture that truly respected the dignity of the individual, CJ could go to his doctor and get a "peaceful pill" for ending his life whenever he chose. This would be CJ's security blanket in old age, respecting a decision to manage his own death. But this was not an option here and now.

And so he began researching his realistic options on the Internet. He was astonished, as he often was online, at how much information was available on methods to kill yourself. He took notes on them all.

"A penny for your thoughts," said Jan.

CJ was sitting in front of a camp fire with the morning's first cup of coffee. He and the Smarts had settled into adjacent campsites at Patagonia Lake, a state park south of Tucson. There was a morning chill in the air.

CJ said, "I made coffee. Help yourself."

Joining him with coffee, Jan said, "Joe is sleeping in."

They were quiet for a while, enjoying the fire and the lake beyond it.

"I think I'll go to Portland," CJ said.

"Oh?"

"I need to see some people."

He wanted to see his best friend, Matt, before he went through with it. Matt was the only person CJ knew who would understand his decision. Molly would have a fit, reason enough to share little with her.

"Are you still on for Mexico?"

They had talked about spending the winter together at Ajijic, an artsy American colony that Joe knew from his youth.

"Why not?"

Of course his plans had changed but he had no desire to get into it with the Smarts. CJ had met them during his first months on the road, five years ago, and they had become his mentors for learning the new rhythm of living in a van. They shared much, the Smarts with careers in academia like himself, Joe also an historian, Jan a Shakespeare scholar.

16

They traveled together often throughout the year. But CJ was not comfortable sharing such a personal decision with them.

He said, "I think I'll head out this morning."

By the time Joe was up and pouring coffee, CJ was packed and ready to go. Jan had moved to her own campsite. CJ came over the say goodbye.

"Did Jan tell you I'm going to Portland?" CJ asked Joe.

"She did indeed. We'll stay in touch to finalize Mexico."

"Sounds good to me."

"Stay upright," said Joe, his habitual farewell.

Jan said, making a theatrical gesture, "Forever, and forever, farewell!"

"Hamlet?" asked CJ.

"Julius Caesar."

Tucson was less than one hundred miles north. CJ was able to get there without a bathroom break. After stopping at a Shell station for fuel and relief, he drove into Tucson and found a sporting goods store.

The hibachis weren't as small as he'd seen on Amazon. His original idea was to rent a compact car for the deed but now he had second thoughts. Two hibachis in the van, set on the floor at opposite ends, should generate enough carbon monoxide for success. This seemed to be the only thing that could go wrong with this method, insufficient generation of CO. He bought two hibachis and a bag of charcoal.

In the van, storing the purchases in a closet, he felt a certain relief. CJ was never one to procrastinate once his mind was made up, but a decision could take considerable time, more so since Helen's death because she always had been the arbitrator of his brooding indecision.

After relief came a sense of empowerment. He was not letting some doctor determine his future. He would manage his own death.

It was almost fifteen hundred miles to Portland. With the driving limitations defined by a bad back, it would take him a week to get there.

2

CJ reached Las Vegas in two days, which he considered a small triumph since he'd cut one day short because of stomach pains. His motel outside of town had an adjacent cafe and free wifi. After breakfast he started reading his email.

Three messages. Jan Smart was just checking in since they hadn't heard from him, making sure he got back on the road without problems. Sometimes Jan acted like a mother.

Molly said that Kayla, her granddaughter, had received a scholarship to graduate school at the University of Washington to study music. CJ had to smile. The bright but troubled young woman had become a friend in Portland, the former teacher still enjoying the company of young people. She had had a rough life and deserved a break.

"You don't know me," the third message began. "My name is Sarah, and your friend Matt is my father. I should say was because Dad died yesterday of a massive heart attack."

CJ stopped reading. His eyes began to swell with tears.

"More coffee, sir?"

The young waitress was holding a pot. CJ nodded.

She poured and said, "Is everything all right?"

"A friend died."

"I'm so sorry."

She offered a smile of condolences, caressed his shoulder and departed.

CJ read on. A memorial service was scheduled in four days. He had no time to dawdle.

CJ Brooding
Makoshika State Park, Montana

Through most of his life, CJ gave no thought whatever to managing his own death. He was too active, too focused on his career and studies, too much in love with Helen, to contemplate dying. But Helen's cancer, and particularly the stressful, frustrating cycle of remission and return, made him conclude that death itself was preferable to such suffering and, to a degree, such victimized manipulation by an overly optimistic medical industry. No, if CJ got cancer, he would do himself in before going through what Helen went through. He would manage his own death.

But he didn't have cancer. Not yet. And thoughts of his own death faded from consciousness.

Such thoughts returned on a late spring afternoon at Makoshika State Park in eastern Montana, less than one hundred miles from the North Dakota border. He sat in a folding chair next to the van, in a campground mostly deserted, with a view of pine and juniper studded badlands stretching to the horizon. Makoshika was a Lakota word meaning bad earth or bad land, and CJ had spent almost an hour hiking with a small group along a trail the ranger called a dinosaur path. He had over-extended himself and was exhausted.

It was in this state of exhaustion, in solitude, facing the barren but beautiful landscape, in Lakota country, that CJ thought, for the first time, how nice it would be to fall asleep in his folding chair now and never wake up. As he lazily lingered on this thought, at first pleasant because it would relieve his exhaustion, he realized how little the world would change if the thought actually came to pass. A few people would miss him, of course, primarily Matt and Molly in Portland, perhaps his new travel buddies Joe and Jan Smart, but he had no family and no legacy except in academia, books and articles about American genocide against the Indians, work few read today. His death would be a disappearance with few consequences and little grief.

This was not a pleasant thought, and CJ was not ready

to embrace it. He changed the subject in his mind and started thinking about what to make for dinner.

3

Driving into Portland, CJ felt no degree of homesickness for the city in which he had lived most of his adult life. He had been gone five years and traffic was twice as bad as he remembered it. Construction was going on everywhere. He saw no changes he liked. As soon as Matt's funeral was over, he'd get the hell out of there. He'd get back on the road and head for the four corners area of the southwest. Monument Valley, the Goose Necks of the San Juan River. The most spiritual landscape in America. Where better to camp, meditate, and ultimately light the charcoal?

CJ's first stop was at the eastside cemetery to pay respects to Helen. He lingered for half an hour, trying to figure out how he felt. He missed her, still, and yet he'd been away from her grave for so long, his marriage and happiness with her felt like they belonged to another life. So much had changed since her death – in his life and routine, in the country, in the world. And so much new change was accelerating in his direction. But at least with the hibachis and charcoal, he felt in charge of his own future. That was the important thing.

Molly was his second stop. She'd gained weight in five years, apparently giving up on her constant struggle to keep it off.

"I was so sorry to read about your friend dying," she said. They were drinking iced tea on her patio. "I didn't realize he was so accomplished."

CJ had known Matt since graduate school, off and on they had played in folk groups together, and they had ended their academic careers as colleagues at Portland State University, Matt in theater arts. He also was a playwright, who had written several well-regarded, controversial plays.

"I didn't even know he had a daughter," said CJ.

"He never mentioned her?"

"Not that I remember. He had a son. I didn't like him. Came on like a back-slapping salesman."

There was a silence.

Molly said, "I assume you'll take the guest bedroom."

"If it's no trouble."

"Of course it's no trouble."

He grimaced from a sudden stab of pain in his gut.

"CJ?"

CJ recovered.

"It's nothing."

"It certainly didn't look like nothing," said Molly.

"Old age."

"Have you seen a doctor?"

CJ shrugged.

"CJ, you're acting like a child. What is going on?"

"I've been getting cramps."

"Abdominal?"

"Stomach, somewhere in there."

"You need to have it looked at."

"I know."

"Well?"

When CJ didn't reply, she said, "I'm going to nag you until you see a doctor."

"I'll call the VA."

"You know where the phone is."

"Now?"

"Before you forget."

"You're acting like my mother."

"Someone has to."

CJ gave in and said, "Okay, okay. I'll phone the VA."

He went through with it to get Molly off his back. He might also get better pain pills that he was buying over the counter. By exaggerating his condition, he managed to get an appointment the day after the memorial service. He wanted to get out of town as soon as possible.

Trump Driving CJ Crazy

"My IQ is one of the highest—and you all know it! Please don't feel so stupid or insecure; it's not your fault."

Donald Trump on Twitter

4

The funeral was not at all what he expected. CJ knew many people there: former colleagues at Portland State, Matt's son Adam, a few of Matt's students that CJ had had in class as well. But there was nothing avant-garde in the ceremony for an avant-garde theater artist, and CJ imagined that Matt himself would have hated it. He guessed the son had arranged it.

Outside the church a woman approached him as he was leaving.

"Pardon me. I'm Matt's daughter, Sarah. I emailed you."

She was a big woman, younger than CJ expected (under 40, he thought), her dishwater blonde hair in a long ponytail. Her granny glasses and black cotton turtleneck suggested a preference for bohemian fashion. She carried a purple tote bag. An Earth Mother, CJ concluded.

"Is there somewhere we could go and talk?"

Over coffee at a nearby Starbucks CJ learned that Sarah was Matt's "love child," and her mother, whom Sarah called the love of Matt's life, was the artist Mary Worthington.

Sarah was waiting for a reaction. CJ got the idea he should recognize the name.

"I don't know much about art," he finally said.

"She's very well known. Especially for her southwest landscapes. Her inspiration was Georgia O'Keeffe."

"Is she still alive?"

"In a matter of speaking. She's diabetic and is going blind, and I think she has early dementia. Or maybe Alzheimer's."

"I'm sorry to hear that," said CJ.

"Don't be. She had an incredible life, and she's taking these changes head on. That's what I want to talk to you about."

"Okay."

"I'm a filmmaker," said Sarah. "Dad was helping me with my new project. We'd always talked about working together, and the project was really important to him. When he got sick earlier in the year, we thought we could finish before he took a turn for the worse. Neither of us expected how bad that turn would be and how soon."

"I was shocked at the news."

Sarah sipped coffee before going on.

"The film is about mother, and dad was going to narrate it. When I asked him to do this, he mentioned you. Too bad CJ left town, he would be perfect. He has a tone of voice filled with moral outrage."

"Sounds like Matt."

"So I was wondering, would you narrate my film?"

CJ almost laughed. Was she serious?

Sarah continued

"I'm almost done shooting. The narration is the last thing I write, of course, but I could be ready to record you in a few weeks, I think. You'd be paid."

"Actually I don't plan to stick around," said CJ.

Sarah leaned closer and the volume of her voice lowered.

"Mother sees no point in living if she's blind. She's decided to take her own life. I'm going to film it."

"Jesus."

The response was automatic and misleading. CJ was not shocked. He was flabbergasted that so soon after his own decision, the possibility of a kindred soul would appear before him, a woman determined to manage her own death.

Sarah said, "She's lighting charcoal in a small closed car. Carbon monoxide poisoning."

"Death by hibachi," said CJ.

"You've heard of it? It was quite the rage in Japan."

Heard of it! CJ felt disoriented, as if some joke by the gods was being played on him, some cosmic coincidence. He was speechless.

Sarah said, "What I'm doing is illegal, of course. This is just between us. Dad trusted you, so I do, too."

CJ was still silent.

"CJ, I have to be able to trust you."

"Yes, of course." He scooted his chair back. "Listen, I think your mother is a courageous woman. I admire what she's doing. But I can't help you, I really do have to get out of town as soon as possible." He stood up. "Good luck with the film."

"Will you at least look at an outline?"

She brought a manuscript out of her purple tote bag.

CJ didn't reach to take it.

"Please read it," she said.

CJ took it.

"My contact info is on the script. I'd appreciate feedback. Dad respected your opinion very much."

"Good luck," he said, and he was out of there.

Methods of Suicide on the Internet
CJ's annotated list

1. Gun Shot. *Too messy. I'd need to learn new skills. Never owned a gun in my life. Never shot one except in Army.*
2. Drug/Alcohol overdose. *Consider. Danger of vomiting.*
3. Hanging. *No confidence I could pull this off. Knots, rope, right location, I don't have right skills.*
4. Poisoning. *Too painful. I have enough stomach cramps already.*
5. Carbon Monoxide Inhalation. *Consider. A variation called Death by Hibachi, popular in Japan.*
6. Suffocation. *Sounds like a trick. Too complicated.*
7. Jumping. *Too messy. Not trying to make a statement. Just want to fade away from my dying planet.*
8. Slitting wrists. *Painful, messy.*
9. Electric shock. *Complicated, painful.*
10. Drowning. *Complicated, too prolonged, unpleasant.*

CJ found the list on the Internet and copied it onto his Kindle Fire tablet. He didn't want to inconvenience others or tax his own physical and mental skills. Something simple, easy, clean, with a high success rate.

It didn't take long for him to select the option that made the most sense to him.

5

In Molly's guest room, CJ stretched out on the bed, brooding. He dozed off. When he awoke, he picked up the book he'd been reading, Richard Hofstadter's Pulitzer Prize study, *Anti-Intellectualism in American Life*.

He'd first read it in graduate school and was returning to it to try and put the Trump phenomenon in historical context after running across a quotation by H. L. Mencken, one he had forgotten about (probably a reference to Harding but sounding contemporary): "On some great and glorious day the plain folks of the land will reach their heart's desire at last, and the White House will be adorned by a downright moron." Mencken had written this in 1920.

Of course! In this light, the new anti-science ignorant President was not an anomaly but another step in a long, unfortunate American tradition. It was easy to forget this tradition because, in fact, CJ wished it were not true. He wished the citizenry was more educated than it was. The election of Trump was a dramatic reminder of the American reality.

He was still reading when Molly opened the bedroom door without knocking.

"I'm sorry," she said. "I didn't know you were home."

"For a while now."

"I thought you'd be at the services longer. Wasn't there a reception?"

"I didn't go."

There was an awkward silence.

Molly said, "I was checking to see if your bed needed to be made."

"You don't have to make my bed."

Another silence.

"Well," said Molly, "I'd better start thinking about dinner. Are you hungry?"

"Starving actually."

"Come watch me cook. I can give you cheese and wine."

"Sounds good."

As CJ sat at the coffee bar, he was tempted to share

with Molly the incredible coincidences he had experienced. He was used to talking to Helen about what was on his mind but he had talked to no one in this way, not even the Smarts, in a very long time. He sipped his wine, nibbled on cheese, and kept his mouth shut, barely listening as Molly went on about one thing and another.

Tomorrow morning he'd go to the VA. By afternoon he hoped to be back on the road. He was eager to get to southern Utah, camp, and get mentally prepared to light the charcoal.

CJ's Reading

When the United States began its national existence, the relationship between intellect and power was not a problem. The leaders were the intellectuals. ... It is ironic that the United States should have been founded by intellectuals; for throughout most of our political history, the intellectual has been for the most part either an outsider, a servant, or a scapegoat.

Richard Hofstadter, *Anti-Intellectualism in American Life*

Trump Driving CJ Crazy

"The concept of global warming was created by and for the Chinese in order to make U.S. manufacturing non-competitive."

Donald Trump on Twitter

6

The visit to the VA changed CJ's plans. The doctor's diagnosis, to be verified with more tests, was prostate cancer.

CJ had not considered the possibility of cancer. Now the doctor was sending him home to wait for the test results. More time in Portland! Moreover, this was another strange coincidence since his profound decision to light the charcoal. Now that it was irrelevant, he might have cancer! CJ's empowerment was throwing surprise after surprise at him.

"I'm not afraid of death," he told Molly that night. Molly had been the first to get the news of possible cancer. He did not share the irony that the news didn't bother him because it had become irrelevant. He was making conversation to terminate Molly's prying about his VA visit. "I'm afraid of dying the way Helen died."

"What are you talking about? You're not going to die. People are surviving cancer all the time."

"Helen didn't."

"They didn't know as much then. They didn't have the technology they have now."

"I don't trust doctors."

"That's juvenile," said Molly.

"Maybe the tests will come out negative."

But they didn't. He had stage two prostate cancer, and they'd caught it before it began spreading, the doctor said. He was eager to start an aggressive treatment plan. CJ said he'd have to think about it, everything was happening too fast, and he hung up.

The reality of prostate cancer struck CJ harder than the possibility of it, despite its still being irrelevant in the context of his decision. Out of curiosity, he read about the disease on the Internet and learned he could live several years with no treatment at all. He found little information about how painful the disease might become if he let it progress.

If he'd learned he had cancer before his decision, what would he have done? Not treatment, surely. He would have lived it out or, perhaps, used the news as a kick in the butt to end up exactly where he was now, with a plan for a peaceful exit from life, suicide by hibachi, at a near time of his choosing, the van parked in the most spiritual landscape in America.

He shared none of this with Molly, who was still bombarding him with optimistic assurances about treatment and the miracles of modern medicine. CJ let her babbling pass by without giving in to an urge to argue with her. He knew she meant well. She just had no idea who he actually was.

That night, having decided to hit the road in the morning, he read the outline of Sarah's film for the first time. And the reading changed everything once again.

CJ Brooding
Buffalo National River, Arkansas

After camping a few days along the Buffalo River, CJ wanted to take a short boat trip but didn't trust his skills in a canoe or kayak. When he saw two college boys launching a raft, he inquired whether he might rent a seat to go along. They offered him a free seat as far as their lunch break, where girlfriends would be waiting to feed them.

The trip along the upper portion of the river was just what he wanted, passing beneath towering bluffs and waterfalls, seeing elk and weasels, floating to a small beach for lunch, after which CJ was driven back to his campsite by a girlfriend as the college boys continued their trip.

Now he sat before a campfire, comfortable in the satisfaction of a good day. Until he felt a sharp pain in his chest.

It went as quickly as it came. CJ sat still, attentive, worried, but except for the frightened jolt of it, he felt fine. Might this have been a small stroke of some kind?

He was 78 with a bad back and arthritis but otherwise in what he considered to be good health. However, he hadn't been to a VA doctor in over a year.

Whatever it was, what if it had been worse? What if it had not killed him but left him paralyzed or otherwise unable to take care of himself? He had no one to step in and help him.

CJ wanted to leave this world with as little fuss and bother to others as possible. A serious stroke would make this impossible. The only alternative was to take charge while he still had the capacity to do so. The alternative was to manage his own death.

And what did this mean? It meant suicide. What else could it mean?

This was America, where a man wanting to manage his own death had no choice but to prepare for his own suicide. This was how "great" America was. He had to do it all alone, and this would be stressful, difficult and illegal.

How does an old man balance continued living with managing his own death?

7

"Sorry I'm late," said Sarah.

CJ had phoned her at night, asking to have morning coffee with her. He had something to tell her that he couldn't relate on the phone.

He said, "Sorry to call so late last night."

"Well, you got my attention. What's up?"

"There are some important things I haven't told you about my situation."

Almost half an hour later, CJ felt that he hadn't done a very good job of explaining himself. He began by telling her about his decision, after Helen's death, to drop out of citizenship because the state of the world was so depressing and stressful, and he saw no solutions in sight. How he'd been living on the road these past five years, where he found a new interest in living by being close to Nature, by photographing it, and by putting the photos on a travel blog. How, in time, this became repetitive and less satisfying. Meanwhile the world got worse, especially the climate crisis, with a denier now in the White House; so that eventually, with no children or grandchildren or family, he saw little point in living much longer. This was not a depressing conclusion because, in fact, he felt like he had been blessed with a good life. But he'd also seen the end of life at its worst with Helen and her cancer, and so he naturally began thinking about alternatives for himself, researching suicide on the Internet, where he found the "death by hibachi" option, which struck him as the most humane and peaceful way he could go since medical assistance was not available, which he considered outrageous. Even immoral. The culture was forcing his only option.

This is why the outline of her film was so moving to him. He had expected to read about her mother's artistic career but this was only the introduction to Sarah's film. The script instead focused on her diabetes and decision to take her own life and her inability to find a doctor who would help her do this. That she ended up choosing death by hibachi, just as CJ had, struck him as some kind of mystical sign. Moreover, that after making his decision he should learn he has cancer, this too felt like a mysterious affirmation that it was time for him to pass, one way or another. He very much wanted to be in charge of what happened, of when and how he would die. Exactly like her mother. He would like to meet her. Moreover, yes, he would be honored to do the narration for her film.

"That's great," said Sarah. "I'm filming tomorrow morning. You could observe, and it would give you the opportunity to meet mother."

"I'd like that."

"Meet me at Sunnyside Place retirement center at nine. Let me write down the address. On the other hand, let's meet at the Starbucks nearby, so we can talk first. It's on the main drag, you can't miss it."

At dinner Molly wanted to talk about his cancer and scheduling treatment. CJ, deciding to be polite, let her talk but his thoughts were elsewhere, with Sarah's film project and all the coincidences that brought him to it.

Finally Molly realized that CJ wasn't going to relieve her concern.

"Okay, I'm done," she said. "So let's talk about something else."

There was a silence.

CJ said, "Do you believe in coincidences."

"No. I believe things happen for a reason. Why?"

"Sarah's film, Matt's daughter, is about how her artist mother has diabetes and is losing her sight and, as an artist, doesn't want to live if she can't see."

Molly said, "Are you implying what I think you are?"

"Don't you think people should be able to manage their own death?"

"Absolutely not. Only God determines when someone should die."

"I didn't realize you were so religious."

"Well, I am. I just don't wear it on my sleeve."

A silence.

"CJ, you're not thinking about things like that, are you?"

"Like what?"

"Like the mother?"

"Managing my own death? Never occurred to me."

"Good."

"Who would want to leave a dying planet with an imbecile in the White House? We have so much to look forward to."

CJ immediately regretted saying this. His cynicism had escaped of its own volition, like a belch.

"What an attitude," said Molly.

They finished dinner with small talk.

"Want to watch a movie?" Molly asked, clearing the table.

"I'm going to read."

"I'll see you in the morning then."

"I have a morning appointment with Sarah."

"Oh?"

She waited for more.

CJ got up.

"Will you be here for lunch?" Molly asked.

"I doubt it."

"Dinner?"

"I expect to."

"Then I'll see you this evening. Goodnight."

CJ's Reading

To the writer who has just eviscerated their way of life and their self-satisfying compromises, readers now say "How interesting!" or even at times "How true!" Such passive tolerance can only be infuriating to a writer who looks beyond the size of his royalties and hopes actually to exert some influence on the course of affairs or to strike a note in the moral consciousness of his time. He objects that serious thinking is received as a kind of diversion and not as a challenge.

Richard Hofstadter, *Anti-Intellectualism in American Life*

8

At Starbucks Sarah got right to the point.

"Sunnyside doesn't know about my film. They think I'm shooting video of residents for YouTube. I am but only as a cover for the other."

"I don't follow," said CJ.

"My plan was to tell them what I was doing but Dad said he didn't think they'd let me interview people about their attitudes toward dying. The hype is all about Golden Years, the best time of your life. So dad had me go to another retirement center first. Sure enough, they wanted nothing to do with it. Talking about death would be too depressing for the residents, they said. So if I was going to shoot my film at Sunnyside, where mother was, I had to do it undercover, which meant getting in the door under false pretenses. Dad came up with the idea. A YouTube channel where the residents could show off their hobbies, give a tour of their apartments, cook a favorite dish, whatever out-of-state relatives would be interested in. Isn't that brilliant? Dad really knows, really knew, how to use the system."

"He did indeed."

"So anyway, today I'm shooting a man's gun collection for YouTube. He's a blowhard and won't stop talking about his hero Trump. But it'll give you a chance to meet mother."

"I'm allergic to Trump," said CJ. "What if we meet after you're done?"

"We could meet for lunch. The food there is actually decent."

"Lunch works."

CJ Brooding
Palo Duro Canyon State Park, Texas

CJ had fallen asleep in his folding chair. It had been a long day, too long as far as he was concerned, because the campground was too crowded and the event which had brought him there with the Smarts, a campground musical pageant called *Texas,* which they'd seen earlier in the evening, had been too long and too boring, despite Jan's enthusiasm for it, before and after the event, and he had returned to his van wanting solitude and determined to go his own way in the morning. Jan Smart could get on his nerves with her theater professor's theatrics and delight in large gatherings. CJ poured himself a drink, sat in his chair outside the van, and hoped the Smarts would let him alone tonight. He fell asleep before he was proven wrong.

Jan woke him, saying, "I don't want you falling into the fire."

Joe handed him a bottle of cold beer. By the second one, CJ was feeling awake and cogent again. He also was feeling a little tipsy.

"Do you ever feel like you're just waiting around for the inevitable?" he asked. "Just filling up space?"

"Heavens no," said Jan. "I'm far too busy and too interested in too many things to have time on my hands. I hope you're not suggesting that you are."

"Now and again I feel this way."

"What about your photo blog?" asked Joe. "You seem interested in that."

"I am. But, I don't know ..."

After a silence, CJ said, "I don't have kids and grandkids like you do. Maybe that's the difference."

"It does help," said Jan.

"I'm not saying I regret my choices," said CJ. "But it does provide roots, a legacy, that I don't have now. Don't mind me. I'm just babbling."

"No, this is important," said Jan. "You once said you were surprised how much beauty is still in the world, in Nature. How many places still seem unspoiled. How fortunate you felt to see them."

40

"Even in Texas," said Joe.

"Even in Texas," CJ repeated. "I think my problem is Trump. It's depressing he has so many supporters."

"Yes, that would depress anyone with half a brain," said Joe.

CJ said, "Blessed are the ignorant because they don't lose any sleep over matters like this."

Jan said, "No, they just put a Trump in the White House and the rest of us have to live with it."

Trump! Make America great again! It drove CJ to despair. Great again? As in, Pursuing a policy of genocide against American Indians? As in, Building a country on the labor of slaves? Or more recently as in, Staging a coup d'etat to murder President Kennedy, who wanted to pursue aggressive policies of mutual existence with the country's communist enemies?

"Ignorance Is Bliss," added Joe.

Jan said, "Don't forget Socrates. The unexamined life is not worth living."

"Interesting point about that," said CJ. "He didn't follow up by saying the examined life therefore *is* worth living."

"He implies it," said Joe.

"Maybe," said CJ. "But what if neither one is worth living?"

"You are in a state," said Jan. "I think we should change the subject."

And she did.

9

After killing an hour, CJ met Sarah in the lobby at Sunnyside Place, a sprawling four-story building that was larger than he expected. Hundreds of retirees must live there.

Sarah led the way to her mother's apartment on the third floor.

"You wait here," she said. "Mother can be moody about meeting new people."

CJ waited outside the apartment. On the hallway walls were paintings by Worthington, landscapes of the very southern Utah area where CJ had planned to spend his final days, paintings in reds, oranges and browns of spectacular rock formations, interpretations that captured the spirituality of the place.

"These paintings are incredible," CJ told Sarah when she returned.

"I'll let mother know you like them. She'll like that. She thinks people have forgotten her."

"She's really good," said CJ.

"Yes, she is. Listen, she's not up to having guests. I need to spend some time with her alone. Why don't you have lunch without me? The dining room is down the hallway and to the right. It's on the house. They're expecting you. After lunch, come back here. Maybe mother will be ready to meet you then."

"I hope so."

"Take your time. Give me an hour."

"See you in an hour," said CJ.

Trump Driving CJ Crazy

"An extremely reliable source has called my office and told me that Barack Obama's birth certificate is a fraud."

Donald Trump on Twitter

10

"Professor Jones!"

CJ was standing inside the dining room, wondering where to sit. He did not expect such a large facility, nor so many residents already sitting at tables. He faced a sea of gray and white hair. Most tables were full, none appeared vacant, and he was wondering whom to join for lunch.

The voice calling his name came from the left, where he saw a man sitting alone at a corner table, waving a raised hand at him. CJ headed that way.

"Come join me," the voice continued.

It belonged to a man who looked younger than most residents there, thin, almost haggard, with a scraggly red beard and unkempt longish hair. He wore jeans and a rumpled, faded blue work shirt. He looked familiar. Especially a certain intensity in his blue eyes. He looked like someone about to spring a practical joke.

"God is red!," the man said, grinning. "God is red!"

A former student? But who?

"Sit your butt down."

CJ sat.

"Are you a former student?" CJ asked.

"Oh, how soon they forget!"

"You look familiar, but I can't quite place you."

Suddenly the man recited, in musical rhythm, his gaze more intense than ever, words from a poem: "As long as you and I have arms and lips which are for kissing and to sing with, who cares if some one-eyed son of a bitch invents an instrument to measure Spring with?"

"The Cummings mantra," said CJ. "I remember."

In class years ago, the student had needed little excuse to recite these lines, no matter the subject at hand. He had put other poetic lines to memory as well and was not bashful about reciting them.

CJ said, "But your name still escapes me."

"Charlie Roberts."

"Yes. You're a writer."

"Once upon a time. Literary refugee is more accurate. I write novels of ideas that bore the mainstream."

"Is that a bad thing?" CJ asked.

"Only when the rent is due."

"How do you manage?"

"I'm a good whore. Sometimes called a Hollywood script doctor. Surreal and lucrative."

CJ remembered more about him.

"You were the life of my classroom," he said. "Always challenging me. That was a long time ago."

"Evening class, 1981. The year *My Dinner With Andre* came out."

"We talked about it in class, as I recall."

"Talked about it! You were obsessed with it. We discussed it for a week. About how we were entering a new Dark Ages. How we had to form pockets of light to save civilization."

"I remember," said CJ softly.

Charlie said, "And look at the country, the world, today. Was Andre right on, or what?"

CJ said, "You were writing about the Whitman Massacre from the Cayuse point of view."

"*Dark Mission*. You do remember!"

"An opera?"

"The libretto."

"Did it get finished?"

"Oh yes. I think it's brilliant but then I'm biased and a huge fan of the composer."

"Has it been performed?"

"Of course not. This is America. It didn't help that my composer had a nervous breakdown and stopped marketing it."

"So do you live here?" CJ asked.

"I, like a few others, am captive here. I'm sorry about your friend Matt, by the way."

"You knew Matt?"

"Not well, but we had lunch together now and again. Very neat guy. He kept me sane here. Hard to find intelligent conversations in a place like this. It's all bingo and card playing and Bible study."

"What do you mean, you're captive here?"

"I had a stroke, my daughter got power of attorney, and she doesn't want me living alone. So here I am, more or less against my will."

45

"Why don't you just leave?"

"I tried. It didn't take long for me to get picked up and returned. My access to my own money is limited."

"That's terrible."

"Actually Matt was going to help me get out of here."

"Really."

"I know about his daughter's film. The real one."

CJ was silent.

Charlie said, "He told me they were moving soon to a new location at a campground on the coast. Since I've made a few digital shorts, maybe I could be useful on the project. I could be a second camera. That would get me out of here without being put out on the street. We'd figure the rest out later. Matt had a really big heart."

"A born idealist," said CJ.

"He was going to talk to Sarah. I don't even know if he had time."

"I'll ask her."

"That would be really great."

A server came by, and they ordered.

"I'm really glad to see you," said Charlie as they waited for food.

"I'm glad to see you again, too."

"Can I get your cell phone number? I'd like to stay in touch."

CJ said, "I don't know it. I seldom use it."

"But you have one?"

"Yes."

It had been a gift from the Smarts, shocked that he didn't have a smart phone. CJ was intimidated by it but liked having it for emergencies on the road.

"May I see it?" Charlie asked. "I'll get your number, and give you mine."

As Charlie was doing something with the phone, CJ said, "Maybe you can show me how to use it."

Charlie laughed.

"I remember your story about your first computer. Once a Luddite, always."

He returned the phone.

"I stand guilty," CJ said. "I'm old school. Less is more."

"Almost your mantra," said Charlie. "So how the hell have you been?"

In this ordinary question, CJ almost found humor. Oh just fine, Charlie, I was on my way to commit suicide in Monument Valley but learned I have prostate cancer, so maybe I'll just let Nature take its course.

He said, "Old and retired. But I will ask Sarah if Matt talked to her about you."

"I really appreciate it. I'm dying in here."

After lunch, CJ learned that Matt indeed had suggested that Charlie Roberts help out on the filming at the campground. Sarah wanted to make sure he could be trusted.

"I believe he can," said CJ. "He's what was called anti-establishment in the sixties."

"I'll talk to him," said Sarah. "Would you be able to come along as well? Being there would give you a feel for the project. I think that would help your narration."

CJ was quiet. What was he getting himself into?

"Unless you have other plans next week."

"Not really."

His plan, so carefully thought out, to beeline to Monument Valley to light the charcoal, had been complicated by cancer and by agreeing to do the narration.

"Then you can come?" asked Sarah.

CJ fidgeted, thinking.

After a hesitation, he said, "Sure."

What would Helen have advised him to do? Alone on the road, he had not missed her as much as now, maneuvering through the ordinary tasks of life.

11

"I don't understand," said Molly. CJ had told her that he was refusing treatment. "You give the impression you want to die."

CJ stared over her shoulder.

"CJ?"

"Does it matter? I don't have a lot of years, no matter what happens."

"But you could live longer with treatment."

He said nothing.

"You scare me," said Molly.

She wouldn't get off the subject, and CJ let his mind drift to Charlie Roberts, the remarkable student who had reentered his life. Their lunch had included exchanging class stories, often leading to laughter, a kind of laughter CJ hadn't experienced in too long, laughter with a kindred soul.

"CJ? Are you even listening to me?"

"I'm sorry."

"What is with you? I think you're more worried about cancer than you admit."

"It isn't that."

"Then what is bothering you?"

"Nothing's bothering me. I just had a nice surprise at lunch. A former student of mine is at the retirement center. One of the most unusual students I've ever had. I can't get him off my mind."

"That sounds like a good thing."

CJ didn't respond.

Molly said, "Isn't he young to be in a retirement center?"

"He was an older student, in a night class, but you're right, he had a stroke much too young."

"How is he?"

"He seems fine physically. His mind is as sharp as ever."

"So he's very bright," said Molly.

"It's more than that. He's unpredictable. He gets you to think about things in a new way, or about something that never occurred to you. He's as widely read as anybody I've known."

"Coming from you, that's quite a compliment."

"Coming from me?"

"You who always has his nose in a book. He must have been a very good student."

"He actually didn't deserve the A I gave him. He's undisciplined and lazy. Too creative for his own good, I used to think. Seeing him today, he has a hell of a lot more intellectual energy than I have."

"That's old age, CJ."

"Partly."

"Mostly."

CJ said, "At lunch I laughed more than I have in a long time."

"Another good thing."

"We'll see."

"What am I going to do with you, Mr. Gloom?"

CJ tried to laugh but it wasn't convincing. The magic with Charlie Roberts did not transfer to Molly.

12

A few days later CJ again had lunch with Charlie at Sunnyside Place, at the former student's invitation. As before, they told war stories from the night class that now was more special than it had seemed at the time. They reminisced about the impact of *My Dinner With Andre,* an early alert about America's new Dark Ages. They shared books they recently had read. And, of course, they compared outrage and laments about the appalling character, ignorance and narcissistic behavior of their president.

"Mencken expected a moron in the White House," said Charlie. "I think Thump fills the bill."

"I remember the famous Mencken quotation," said CJ, "but I still was shocked."

"But Mencken was a snob. Elitist, they'd say today. He didn't believe in the nobility of quote The People unquote. But even he may have underestimated the stupidity factor."

CJ said, "The last person believing in the nobility of the People may have been Woody Guthrie. What's your theory?"

"I don't do theories. I just make observations, hopefully related to reality."

"Remember what your man Cummings wrote about them?"

"Oh yes. A politician is an arse upon which everyone has sat except a man."

CJ said, "Divide and rule, the politician cries! Goethe."

"What is this, Beat that Quotation? I was really too honest a man to be a politician and live. Socrates. Remember what Aristophanes listed as the characteristics of a good politician?"

"Remind me," said CJ.

"A horrible voice, bad breeding and a vulgar manner."

"This conversation makes me want to cry."

"And that's exactly what's wrong with us," said Charlie. "The so-called educated class. We are blinded by the small immediate event and forget that in the long run this, too, whatever it is, shall pass. We're always focusing on bad news and ignore good news."

"Climate change won't pass," said CJ. "We're doomed."

"True enough. But the real question is, OK, the ship is sinking. What do we do in the meantime? Abandon ship? Jump overboard?"

"In a manner of speaking, that's exactly what Mary Worthington is doing, isn't it?"

"But she's motivated by old age and her personal circumstances, not climate change or politics. For her, suicide is empowering, not desperate."

"That's true," said CJ.

"Have you read Susan Jacoby's book on the myth of a new old age?"

"No. I like her *The Age of American Unreason* very much. A good update of the Hofstadter classic."

"I'm done with my copy. I'll send you home with it."

"I appreciate it."

They ate in silence for a moment.

Charlie said, "As long as you and I have arms and lips which are for kissing and to sing with ... We so-called 'serious thinkers' get so blinded by current events and our theories that we forget personal passion. That's the Achilles heel of the intellectual. We can't see the trees for the forest. Trump may be President but guess what, Billie Holiday still sings to me!"

"Until he bans her."

"That's a depressing thought," said Charlie.

"But with Trump, it could happen. I think he'll declare martial law before he's gone."

Sarah entered the dining room and walked to their table.

CJ asked, "How's your mother?"

"Better. Chomping at the bit. We leave tomorrow morning."

Trump Driving CJ Crazy

"In addition to winning the Electoral College in a landslide, I won the popular vote if you deduct the millions of people who voted illegally."

Donald Trump on Twitter

CJ's Reading

... health gurus, online and offline, who suggest that lifestyle changes can somehow produce a "real age" that is more real than one's biological age are really selling snake oil.

Susan Jacoby, *Never Say Die: the Myth and Marketing of the New Old Age*

PART TWO

Death, Thy Rhythmic Lover
E. E. Cummings

CJ Brooding
Molly's guest room, Portland

Waking with cramps, CJ entertained the notion of calling the whole thing off. He already had begun to question his original plan in the new context of his cancer. If he had only several years to live without treatment, why not just let nature take its course? At least until he felt more discomfort than occasional abdominal cramps. He could live with this.

He also had second thoughts about narrating Sarah's film. He believed in what she was doing, still, but he had abandoned citizenship for a reason. Now he was becoming politically active again by his participation in the film. Was this really what he wanted to do? The stress of activism already was returning. The trouble with having a cause was that it might fail. This possibility was stressful. He was an old man. Hadn't he already done enough for progressive causes?

He also was physically tired. His old age knew nothing about second winds, renewed energy. He had been tired yesterday, he was tired today, and he would be tired tomorrow. Driving to the southwest to go through with his plan seemed as daunting as running a marathon. He just wanted to rest. He just wanted to keep still.

But his mind wouldn't shut off. He knew it was nearing time to get up and meet Sarah at Sunnyside Place. He said he would narrate her film. Why was it so hard to get out of bed? Why was his stomach acting up again? Stress, CJ decided. He was letting stress back into his life.

The bedroom door opened.

"Do you want breakfast before you go?" Molly asked.

"I don't have time but coffee would be nice."

"It's already on."

This got him out of bed and dressed. At the coffee bar, he said, "I'll be back in a day or two."

He wasn't sure how long the filming would take. The filming! Actually Mary Worthington was committing suicide. "The filming" didn't quite cover it.

"I'll be here," said Molly.

Then, by the plan, he would head for the southwest, bailing the narration. Or maybe not. Maybe he should relax

57

and stay a while right where he was. Read, listen to jazz, do nothing. Except when she acted like his mother or made romantic overtures, Molly was pleasant enough to be around.

"You look tired," said Molly.

"I am."

"This is something you have to do?"

"I said I'd help. I'm a man of my word."

"That you are. Forgive me if I worry about you."

CJ almost said, At least someone is. He didn't because there was a chance Molly would misinterpret it.

"Well, I'm on my way," he said and took a final sip of coffee.

13

Sarah led the way in her VW with her mother and mother's friend, Gladys, who had terminal leukemia and talked Sarah into joining them. CJ followed in the van, Charlie Roberts riding shot gun. Mary Worthington had chosen their destination, Beverly Beach State Park near Newport, a two-and-a-half hour drive, first south to Salem and then west to the coast. Younger, Mary had camped there often, and Sarah remembered camping there as a child.

CJ finally had met the artist at Sunnyside as they prepared to leave and was taken aback by how frail and unresponsive the old woman was. Her comments, in a soft voice he barely could hear, struck CJ as random, unattached to conversation, and he wondered if this were a result of the early dementia Sarah had described. More than once, and without context, Mary had said, "I miss purple mornings ..." CJ had told her how much he admired her paintings but Mary made no response, if his remark even registered with her. She was in her own world. Gladys, in contrast, was cogent, if even more physically frail than her friend, clearly dying.

Charlie brought along a ukulele, which he pronounced OO-kah-lay-lee. CJ considered this a bit strange, considering the purpose of their trip, but said nothing until they had been on the freeway for a while.

"What's with the ukulele?"

"What do you mean?"

"It strikes me as a little out of place, considering our purpose."

The purpose, to die with dignity by voluntary suicide, already had become more stressful than earlier, when it all seemed like so much theoretical talk. Now they were on their way to turn theory into action. Not one but two old women were committing suicide!

Charlie said, "On the contrary! Sarah told me she wants the mood to be like a wake. A farewell wake, she called it. So I thought a little music would be appropriate."

They drove a few miles in silence.

CJ said, "I used to play in a folk trio with Matt. Weavers, labor songs. So what kind of music do you play?"

"Fiddle tunes, clawhammer style, and jazz."

"On the uke? Amazing."

"I'm just average. You should check out YouTube. There are incredible ukulele players out there."

"I always associated the uke with Tiny Tim."

"An unfortunate legacy."

A few more miles.

"I'm glad we connected again," said Charlie. "I enjoy your company."

The feeling was mutual.

14

CJ was impressed with how much planning Sarah had done. At Beverly Beach State Park, she led the way to a secluded campsite at the edge of the coastal forest. Her own tent would accommodate the three of them who would not be expressing their last rights. She had an extra sleeping bag for Charlie, and CJ would use his own.

Earlier, stopping at a market outside the campground, Sarah had purchased cans of Dinty Moore Beef Stew, peanut butter and bread, a few deli items. They sat at the camp table and ate sandwiches for lunch, then Sarah set up one camera on a tripod and gave the hand-held to Charlie. She called for attention, ready to give opening remarks that Charlie would film.

"We're going to do this in three parts," she began.

CJ took a deep breath, wondering how heavy this would get. Sarah's tone didn't suggest an emotional context but for CJ the day already felt different from what he expected, certainly more anxious, despite his agreement in principle to the imminent suicides. His stomach cramps were acting up, and CJ had neglected to get prescribed pain pills at the VA. He only had a few over-the-counter pills left, and they didn't always provide relief.

Sarah continued: "We begin with what I am calling a farewell wake. In essence, it's a celebration. In particular, a celebration of the individual lives of my mother and of Gladys. I hope both will share with us some highlights of their remarkable lives. What are the experiences you have never forgotten? What are the things that made life worth living for you? Again, the emphasis here is celebration, a celebration of life. What we are doing is not driven by depression or desperation. We do what we do because we have no choice, the medical industry has given us no choice, they have let us down, inhumanely so, and in a saner world we would be doing this quite differently. But here we are, left to make do with the reality of American culture. We are doing the best we can under the circumstances."

Charlie asked, even as he continued filming, "Can everybody participate in this celebration of life?"

"I hadn't considered that. You have something you want to say?"

"Absolutely. I celebrate life every day."

"Okay. Anyone can share who wants to. Any other questions?"

"Why can't we see the ocean?" Mary asked.

"The ocean is a short hike away. Under the highway tunnel. We can see it later. I wanted us to be as secluded as possible."

"When my daughter was little," Mary began. She looked confused. "Are you my daughter?"

"Yes, mom, it's Sarah."

"Sarah."

Mary stopped. She looked lost.

"Mom? You were saying when I was little ..."

"Did I? I can't remember what I wanted to say."

"I always wanted to camp where we could see the ocean. But this is different. We don't want to draw any attention to what we're doing. OK?"

"I don't think the morning is purple any more," said Mary.

Sarah smiled, a touch sadly in CJ's opinion, and said, "I'm going to continue. So the first stage is a celebration of life. This will take up most of the afternoon. We may take a break to walk on the beach. I think the ocean is a perfect metaphor, an image, for the enormity of what we are doing here. Death is part of the cycle of life, and we're acting in tune with the universe. Of course, we could be arrested, but that's a condemnation of American culture, not of ourselves. Consider, for example, how other cultures deal with death."

Sarah stopped and spoke to Charlie.

"This next sequence is important. I want you to shoot it really close."

Charlie made an adjustment on the lens.

Sarah continued.

CJ Brooding
Beverly Beach State Park, Oregon

In late afternoon, Sarah decided everyone needed a break. Those who wanted could walk on the beach, or hike in the woods, and those who needed it could take a nap in the van or in the tent.

Mary and Gladys chose to nap in the tent. Charlie said he was staying in camp to practice the ukulele. He'd never been filmed playing before and was nervous. Sarah invited CJ to stroll on the beach.

"When will I be recording the narration?" CJ asked after they had walked a while.

"I'll start writing as soon as I can, but a lot depends on what happens tomorrow. Are you in a hurry?"

"I'm eager to get back on the road."

The response was automatic. In fact, he was still confused about what to do.

Sarah said, "You realize we may all be arrested, don't you?"

"I hadn't thought about it."

"You should. Is something else bothering you?"

"I guess I'm just restless."

"Well, you're in the loop. You'll know what I know."

They walked in silence.

Sarah said, "I'm heading back. I have prep to do. I'll want to start in about an hour."

"I'll be there."

"You can always leave, CJ."

"No, I'll be there."

Farther on, CJ sat on a log and stared up and down the beach, seeing only a few people in small scattered groups along the long stretches of sand. In the distance a dog raced between two couples. The rhythm of waves gave the afternoon a meditative soundscape.

He found himself thinking of Helen. Some sixty years ago, on a beach much like this one, she had led him into his sexual awakening. He hadn't thought of this in ages. He hadn't missed her so much since his last days in Portland, before hitting the road for distraction and a new life. Now his

63

vagabond life, too, was coming to an end, but on his own terms, not some doctor's, not in accordance with some religious authority. He was taking charge of his own death. But how exactly?

Here, on the brink of witnessing two actual suicides, theoretical empowerment was tempered by immediate grief. And also by anger, because this entire enterprise should be unnecessary and, in fact, would be in a culture giving more than compromised law to the principle of death with dignity. How great was America? It forced Mary and Gladys, and later would force CJ himself, to break the law in order to control the circumstances of their passing.

The ocean continued its rhythmic soundscape. It occurred to CJ that Nature couldn't care less about how humans managed their demise.

15

Sarah continued.

"If you look at the big picture, and at how many other cultures deal with death, our own fear and determination to silence discussion of it clearly come off as atypical, if not paranoid, escapist, delusional. For example, let me read you something I found on the Internet about Buddhism:

"'Buddhist teachings explain that the best spiritual practitioners are joyful when they are dying, as if they're going home to see their family after a long absence. Less accomplished practitioners are happy and comfortable at the time of death and are fully confident that they will have a happy rebirth. And even the least accomplished practitioners die without worry or fear; death does not bother them at all.'"

Sarah paused, as if giving everyone time to let this sink in.

"Wow," she said. "How different is that from how we die in the west, and how we're forced to come here to be able to die with some kind of dignity?"

She gave other examples, from Hinduism, from Islam, from a few religions CJ was not familiar with, but she was over-playing her hand, he thought, talking after she'd quickly made her point. CJ found himself feeling sleepy, bored.

"I think we all need a break," said Sarah at last. "How about we regroup in an hour or two?"

CJ's Reading

The prevalence of Alzheimer's doubles in every five-year period over age sixty-five. These statistics cannot be cited often enough.

Susan Jacoby, *Never Say Die: the Myth and Marketing of the New Old Age*

The celebration of life began after dinner. They'd eaten early, so Sarah could film for as long as possible before darkness. CJ noticed that Mary and Gladys barely ate at all.

Sarah invited everyone to share their greatest passions, whatever made life most worth living. Everything would be filmed.

"OK then," she began. "I'll be first. What makes life worth living? Woody Allen asked himself this very question in one of his movies. His answer? A number of things. Listening to Louis Armstrong's recording of Potato Head Blues. Watching Groucho Marx. Or Marlon Brando. Or Willie Mays. Listening to the second movement of the Jupiter symphony."

As Sarah continued, CJ's mind wandered to Helen again. He was thinking, of all things, of their first kiss. This had been in grad school at the University of Oregon. Matt had talked them into going with him to a summer solstice celebration at the Stonehenge replica overlooking the Columbia Gorge on the Washington side. Most of the revelers were Matt's friends from Seattle. Knowing none of them, CJ and Helen had spread their sleeping bag some distance away from the party. It was here, stretched out as the sky darkened and stars slowly appeared above them, that Helen rolled toward him and instigated their first kiss, and CJ decided he was in love with her.

"That's when I knew I would be a filmmaker," Sarah was saying. "So those are some of the reasons I find life worth living. Who wants to be next?"

"I'll be next," said Charlie.

"I'll be short and sweet," said Charlie. He played a short jazz riff on his ukulele. CJ was impressed. "First, I have profound admiration for our guests of honor, Mary and Gladys. That's how I think of them. This is a celebration of courage in the face of institutional inhumanity, and they are the guests of honor. I'm not sure I could do what you're doing, ladies. I stand in awe of your courage."

He made a quick strum, as if for emphasis.

"We live in a culture in which all the social and political forces at hand focus on us for one purpose: to mold us into customers. Consumers. They are creating a new species, homo consumerus. Homo consumerus.

"What makes life worth living? For me the answer is easy. To resist these forces. To refuse to live as homo consumerus. To refuse to die as homo consumerus. To live my life simply, carefully, aware of every moment because there are temptations everywhere. We face an assault against the species and an assault against the mind.

"As long as you and I have arms and lips which are for kissing and to sing with, who cares if some one-eyed son of a bitch invents an instrument to measure Spring with?"

He played another riff.

"Thank you very much."

CJ spontaneously stood up and applauded. Everyone looked at him.

"Who's next?" asked Sarah. "CJ?"

"I pass."

"Are you sure?"

"I pass."

CJ avoided eye contact with Charlie.

Gladys spoke slowly, softly, but deliberately.

"Ever since Harry's death, I've lived for my grandchildren and great grandchildren. Mostly the little ones. They are so cute then. Before they become teenagers and have to deal with everything. Drugs, bullying, sex, it's all so complicated at that age. So different from when we were young.

"Harry was my rock, but he would've had a hard time with my leukemia. It's a blessing he went first and didn't have to suffer. He would suffer more for me than for himself.

"I made life worth living by keeping busy. A lot was routine, cleaning house and stuff, but there were things that especially gave me pleasure, like baking pies. I baked not only for the family but for friends, who seemed to enjoy them. I knitted and crocheted. I belonged to a bridge club for almost thirty years."

As Gladys went on, CJ realized he could be listening to the story of his mother, and of many American housewives everywhere, who found their meaning in creating a home for family. How many of them had examined their lives in the manner demanded by Socrates? Did it even matter? He recalled an argument with the Smarts about this, in which CJ questioned whether the examined life was any more meaningful than the unexamined life. The Smarts were not convinced.

Gladys said, "When I was diagnosed with leukemia, what upset me was the waiting afterwards, that I couldn't pass as soon as I accepted God's plan for me. What was the point of waiting?

"This is why I decided to use the death with dignity law, so I could control the timing. But when I heard Mary was denied the same opportunity, and that her daughter was making a film about it, to protest this, that's when I asked if I could be a part of it. Mary has every right to die with dignity as much as I do. Let me tell you, once the doctor gave me my dose, I felt like a great weight had been lifted off my soul. The uncertainty disappeared."

Gladys stopped and cleared her throat.

Sarah asked, "What did you and Harry like to do together?"

"We danced at the American Legion. We loved that. Harry was an excellent dancer. Much better than me.

"And travel. Once the kids were grown and out of the house, we bought an RV and traveled quite a bit in Harry's last years. Harry always wanted to move on sooner than I did. I liked to find a beautiful spot and just stay there for a while. Harry liked to keep moving."

After a pause, Gladys said, "I guess that's all I have to say."

"Thank you," said Sarah. "Mom, are you up to this?"

19

Even before Sarah, after sitting close to her mother and conversing quietly for a long moment, announced she would film Mary privately in the van, CJ had been worried about the old woman. During the filming of others, Mary exhibited a confused agitation, unable to sit still, frequently glancing up at the sky as if looking for something there, frowning one moment and softly giggling the next. Her dementia appeared to be getting worse right before his eyes. CJ worried that she might not know what was going on. If this were true, the context of her suicide no longer was heroic, or even clear. CJ worried that Sarah was putting her mother up to this.

"Does Mary seem right to you?" CJ asked Charlie after the two women had disappeared into the van. Sarah took the hand-held camera that Charlie had been using. Gladys had excused herself into the tent to rest.

"She seems nervous," said Charlie. "Not that I blame her."

"Do you think she knows what she's doing?"

"Of course she does. You don't?"

"She seems lost to me. I'm not sure she knows what's going on."

"All of this was her idea," said Charlie. "Wasn't it?"

"I don't know."

"That's the impression I had."

"According to Sarah, it was."

"What are you implying?"

CJ said, "I'm confused. Mary is totally out of it, and Sarah carries on like it's just another day at the office. She just lost Matt. She's about to lose her mother."

Charlie thought a moment and said, "Maybe the film is the only thing holding her together."

After a silence, CJ asked, "Do you know what we're going to do with the bodies?"

"I hadn't thought of that."

"Has anyone?"

"I assume Sarah has. I assume she'll call the police tomorrow."

"Then what? We get arrested for murder?"

71

Charlie was silent.

CJ said, "This is a grandiose theory of existential empowerment or something, but I don't see that Sarah or anyone else has thought through the details."

"You could ask her."

"Maybe I will."

20

His opportunity came as Charlie was filling two hibachis with charcoal. When CJ learned Sarah planned to put the women in her car, he had volunteered his van and suggested two hibachis. The van would be much more comfortable for them.

"Where's Sarah?" CJ asked.

"In the tent."

He entered without announcement and found Sarah crying. Or she seemed to be crying.

But she quickly recovered and said, "Goddamn pollen is killing me."

CJ hadn't noticed any pollen.

"I need to talk to you a minute," he said.

"What's on your mind?"

"What do we do with the bodies?"

"I'll call the police in the morning," she said, "and then they'll probably arrest us."

"You want to be arrested?"

"Of course. The whole point is to make the issue as public as possible."

CJ looked surprised by her reply.

Sarah said, "If you don't want to be arrested, you'd better leave now. We can do this in my car."

CJ felt like he was put on the spot. He wasn't sure what he wanted to do.

"I was just wondering," he said.

Sarah led the way out of the tent. Both hibachis were ready.

"How is everybody feeling?" Sarah asked.

CJ made an involuntary sound, almost a verbal smirk. How the hell did she expect him to feel? He was about to witness two suicides.

Sarah said, "I want to remind you again why we are doing this. ..."

CJ saw that Charlie was filming everything. He wished he were stretched out on the bed in Molly's guest room, reading, listening to jazz, napping. He was mentally exhausted.

Sarah said, "Are we all on the same page?"

Gladys and Charlie nodded. Mary stared off into space. CJ took a deep breath, feeling a little light headed.

"Then we'll light the charcoal," said Sarah.

21

Later, in a sleeping bag in the tent, CJ couldn't shut off his mind. Charlie was snoring. Sarah was breathing heavily. CJ was still awake. At least his stomach pain had subsided.

He kept listening for sounds from the van. He half-expected screams or pounding on interior walls, a loss of courage at the last minute by an old woman who had changed her mind, now in panic to remain alive. But he heard nothing.

He wasn't sure how much time had passed since Mary and Gladys had entered the van. CJ had expected a formal ceremony of some kind, a solemn sending off of the women to their fate, but hugs and private whispers replaced formality.

When the van door was closed, Sarah announced that she was going for a walk. She didn't invite anyone to go with her.

Charlie said, "I see what you mean. This feels a lot heavier than the theory of it."

"I'm having a hard time handling it," said CJ.

"What else would you have them do?"

"Nothing. It's not them. It's me. I shouldn't have come."

"I think Sarah appreciates your being here."

After a silence, Charlie said, "I'm turning in."

"I'll be right behind you."

CJ took a short walk along a path through the woods. He headed back when he felt chilly.

By the time CJ entered the tent, Charlie was snoring. A short time later Sarah entered and quietly slipped into her sleeping bag. Soon she was breathing heavily.

Some time later, after finally falling asleep, CJ stirred and saw flashing lights through the canvas walls of the tent. He slipped out of the sleeping bag and opened the front flap.

Three police cars had pulled into the campsite. Several officers had rushed to the van and slid open the door.

Sarah sat up.

"What the hell is going on?"

Charlie coughed and leaned up on an elbow.

"Is somebody here?"

CJ was the first to come out of the tent.

Seeing him, an officer yelled, "Everyone is under arrest!"

22

For what seemed longer than it was, CJ and Sarah waited in the back seat of a police car, locked in, until finally an ambulance arrived, then watching as the women were carried from the van. Were they dead or alive? It was impossible to tell.

Charlie was gone. Either the police officers had not noticed him or decided not to pursue him as he ran off into the woods.

There was another long wait before two policemen entered the car.

Sarah said, "Why are we being arrested?"

The officer riding shotgun said, "Because you think you're God."

PART THREE

And death shall have no dominion.
Dead men naked they shall be one
With the man in the wind and the west moon;
Dylan Thomas

CJ Brooding
Lincoln County Jail, Newport

CJ awoke with a headache but his stomach was fine. What time was it? He had no idea. Daytime. He was alone in a small cell. He listened for evidence that someone, Sarah, might be in a nearby cell.

"Hello?" he said.

Down the way a male voice said, "Shut the fuck up, asshole."

He sat up on the bed. He rubbed his forehead.

What was he being charged with? No one had told him. Playing God, an officer had said in the police car at the campsite.

Did this mean he would be charged with murder? Were the women dead?

He should have listened to his recent doubts about participating. Maybe Sarah, presumably in another cell, would appreciate the publicity surrounding such a serious charge, but this is not what CJ had in mind. He wanted his solitude back. He wanted to mind his own business.

CJ stretched out again. He dozed off.

"Carlton Jones?"

An officer stood at the cell door. He was opening it with a key.

CJ sat up.

"That's me."

"You got bail."

CJ was confused.

"What time is it?"

"A little after three."

Afternoon, thought CJ. He had been there for quite a few hours.

He stood up and stretched.

"Follow me," the officer said.

81

23

"It was on the morning news," Molly explained. They were walking to her car. "I about had a heart attack when I heard your name."

"I appreciate what you're doing," said CJ, "but you really shouldn't have gone to so much trouble." Newport was over a two-hour drive from Portland.

"What are friends for?"

They reached the car and got in. They were on the highway before CJ said, "You are a good friend. Thank you."

"I'm not going to press you about what's going on," said Molly. "But I think I deserve to know. Whenever you're ready."

CJ was ready by dinner, gaining a bit of courage from several glasses of wine as he sat at the breakfast bar, watching Molly cook.

"I think I told you Sarah's mother is an artist," CJ began, "and quite good, but she was going blind and didn't want to keep living but she couldn't get any medical help with the Death With Dignity law, so she decided to take her own life. Sarah was filming it as part of a documentary film on the issue of dying rights."

Molly looked aghast.

"And you went along with this?"

CJ took a deep breath. How much more should he tell her? She had made a good point: she deserved to know what was going on. She was a good friend. Maybe the only real friend he had left. All the same ...

CJ said, "I have no problem with what she is doing."

Molly said, "Fine. I'm doing dishes.

"I'll help."

"I'd rather do them alone."

24

CJ's van had been confiscated as evidence. He had a court date in Lincoln County in the middle of next week. He still didn't know what he was being charged with, if anything. He did know he needed a lawyer.

"I know someone very good," Molly said the next morning. Her earlier anger was gone or hidden. "I don't think she's retired yet. I haven't seen her since her mother's funeral. You tell her exactly what you told me about having second thoughts once you got there."

"I don't want to leave Sarah out on a limb by herself."

"Well, you don't want to sacrifice yourself for her either, do you?"

CJ didn't reply.

"Do you?" Molly asked again.

"I made a commitment to her."

"To narrate her film, right? Not to be charged with murder."

"It wasn't murder."

Now it was Molly's turn not to reply.

CJ said, "How do I get in touch with this lawyer?"

CJ's Reading

... insistence that depression is not a part of "normal" aging—
like the assertion that dementia is not a part of normal aging—
is a ubiquitous feature of the happy talk promoting the myth
of a new old age.

Susan Jacoby, *Never Say Die: the Myth and Marketing of the
New Old Age*

25

The next morning Molly drove CJ to the lawyer's office downtown. On the elevator to the tenth floor, CJ said, "I hope she's not too expensive."

"I can always help out," said Molly.

"I won't accept it."

"You silly man."

Molly led the way into the office. CJ stood back, letting Molly take charge. This was happening a little too fast for him.

The secretary excused herself and went into the private office. When she returned, a thin redhead in a green dress followed her, the lawyer, Ann Watkins.

"Molly!"

They embraced.

Molly said, "This is Carlton."

"CJ," he said and offered his hand.

"Let's go into my office," said Ann. To Molly she said, "You wait here."

When the office door was closed, CJ said, "Molly is pushing me into this. I'm not even sure I need a lawyer. I haven't been charged with anything that I know of. And I can't afford an expensive one. I'll be up front about that."

"Sit down," said Ann. She sat down at her desk. "It's your lucky day. I'm about to retire and if you do need a lawyer, and decide I'm the one, this will be pro bono."

"Really?"

"I need some good karma. A personal matter. So, tell me why Molly thinks you need a lawyer."

Where to begin? He had no idea how much of the story she needed to know.

Ann said, "Begin at the beginning, if you're stuck."

"This will be confidential?"

"Of course."

Okay. CJ took a deep breath. Here we go.

He gave her a short version of events, from deciding to manage his own death, to Matt dying and meeting his daughter Sarah, to deciding to work on her film, then to having second thoughts about it. And the raid by the police at the campground, of course.

"Do you know how the police found out?" Ann asked when a long pause told her CJ was done.

"No idea."

"Okay. Let me contact the sheriff in Lincoln County and see where they are with this and if charges are impending. That's a start. I'll want to see the autopsies as well. You're sure the women died?"

"Not at all. I just saw them carried out to the ambulance."

"Well, there's a lot to find out. It will take me a few days."

"I really appreciate this."

Ann buzzed her secretary.

"Will you have Molly join us?"

While they waited, Ann said, "I have something to say to both of you."

Molly entered and sat in the chair next to CJ.

Ann said, "I'll start getting some details, and we'll see where we stand."

"That's great," said Molly, smiling at CJ.

"As I told CJ, I'll do this pro bono. I need the karma. Molly, you may recall at the funeral that I had just beaten ovarian cancer."

"I do remember. That was wonderful."

"Well, it's returned with a vengeance, and there's really no point in more treatment. So I'm planning to retire and travel while I have a chance. This will be my last case."

Molly said, "I don't know what to say."

"I gave it a good fight for a long time. I feel blessed to get this far."

CJ said, "Maybe you should do that traveling now rather than take the case."

"No, I need the good karma. I believe in stuff like that. So I'll make some calls today and let you know where we stand as soon as I can."

As they stood up to go, Molly said, "Maybe you can be an inspiration to CJ. He's refusing treatment."

"Pardon me?" said Ann.

"He has prostate cancer," said Molly.

CJ glared at her.

"Treatment is an individual choice," said Ann. "When I started treatment, I was, what?, twenty or thirty years younger

86

than CJ is. At his age, diagnosed for the first time, I'm not sure what I would have done."

CJ wanted to change the subject. He said, "I really am wondering now if the women died at all."

Ann said, "I'll get right on in."

On the drive back to Molly's, CJ said, "You didn't have to tell her I have cancer."

"I assumed you would have."

CJ let it rest at that. When they got home, he went into his bedroom and closed the door.

CJ's Reading

It is, in my view, much more rational to contemplate suicide at a time when one still has the capacity to act than it is to simply deny the terrible fate that awaits everyone with Alzheimer's, thereby condemning oneself through inertia to months or years of institutional care.

Susan Jacoby, *Never Say Die: the Myth and Marketing of the New Old Age*

26

CJ had fallen asleep on the bed with the book on his lap. His cell phone rang.

It took him a moment to remember how to answer it. Tap the green phone icon.

"Hello?"

"Hey, it's Charlie! You sound asleep. Are you in jail?"

"Charlie!"

CJ sat up.

"Where are you?" he asked.

"Are you in jail or what?"

"A friend bailed me out. Where are you?"

"At a shelter in Portland. My daughter is trying to find me, I'm sure. I think she plans to tighten the screws. I need a place to lay low for a while. Can you help me?"

CJ thought a moment.

"Professor?"

"Let me ask Molly. Where I'm staying. Can I call you back?"

"That would be great. Can you make it quick?"

"What's your number?"

"I put it in your phone. Look under contacts."

"I hope I can figure it out."

"Can your friend help you?"

"Right. She'd know how to find it. Listen, I'll talk to her right now. I'll call back in a few minutes."

"Thanks, professor."

If Molly had reservations about having another house guest, CJ couldn't read it in her manner. She said anything he wanted to do was fine.

"We'll come pick you up." CJ told Charlie on the phone.

"You've gone to enough trouble. Give me the address. I'll get there."

"Are you sure?"

"I need to be as independent as possible. Give me the address."

But an hour passed and then another. No Charlie.

Molly said, "When did your friend say he was coming?"

"He didn't actually. I assumed right away."

That evening, excusing herself for the night, Molly said, "You have strange friends."

CJ gave up on Charlie around ten and went to bed himself.

27

The next morning CJ was wakened by Molly.

"I think your friend may be on the patio," she said.

CJ found Charlie curled up on the concrete, asleep.

"Charlie?"

Movement.

"Charlie!"

Charlie looked up.

"Hey, professor. What time is it?"

"Something after seven. Were you out here all night?"

"Arrived late. Didn't want to disturb you."

Inside over coffee, Charlie poured on the charm, complimenting so many particulars of Molly's home – the layout of the kitchen with its island stove, the assortment of pots hanging from the ceiling, the hand-crafted coffee cups, the colorful abstract posters on the wall -- that she finally said, "Oh quit it. You don't have to butter up to me to be welcome here."

Charlie laughed.

"The lady tells it like it is."

"She does indeed," said CJ.

Molly scrambled eggs, fried hash browns and bacon, and made another pot of coffee. While she made breakfast, CJ and Charlie went out to the patio to speak privately.

"I have another favor to ask," said Charlie. "I found a blank check in my wallet. It's old but it's the same account. I want to write you a check to see if it goes through."

His daughter, CJ remembered, had power of attorney and had taken all of Charlie's credit cards.

"You think it will bounce?" CJ asked.

"I have no idea how the legal part of this works. Maybe there's a hold on my account, maybe she put all the money into her own account. I know before I had my stroke, I had almost ten grand in it."

"That's a lot of money to lose, if you lost it."

"I don't think she's stealing from me. I think she just doesn't trust me to manage my own affairs. Anyway, how about I write it for five grand?"

"And if it goes through?"

"Give me the money, man!"

They laughed.

CJ said, "This actually isn't funny."

"But laughing keeps us sane. It's becoming the only thing that does."

Molly stepped out and called, "Breakfast is ready!"

"I'm starving," said Charlie.

They went inside.

28

For a few days the household settled into a quiet routine. CJ and Charlie spent a lot of time reading. Molly did what she usually did: puttered around the house, went to a yoga class, visited friends. At meals CJ and Charlie would laugh about things they had shared at the university. Now and again Molly tried to be a part of their reminiscences – she, too, had memories of college classrooms – but clearly they were in their own world. Intellectuals, she realized, marched to a different beat.

Finally news from the lawyer came: Ann said there was too much to share on the phone, and CJ made an appointment to come to her office that afternoon.

"She didn't give you any details?" Molly asked.

"Just that it's all good news. Including getting my van back."

"Did the women survive?" Charlie asked.

"She didn't say."

"Do you think I could pick her brain for some free advice? Or doesn't she seem like the type?"

CJ said, "I think she might be open to a few questions. You want to come along?"

Molly said, "You two take the car. I don't need to be your chauffeur."

On the drive to the lawyer's office, Charlie said, "You nervous?"

"A little."

"After I ran off, I felt guilty."

"Well, I guess it doesn't really matter now. She said it's all good news."

And it was, to a surprising degree. The women had died, yes, but the autopsies revealed that it wasn't carbon monoxide that had killed them. Each had ingested secobarbital, which had killed them. Gladys Holt, Ann learned, had been given a vial by her doctor to use for herself, having used the Death With Dignity law to obtain it. Apparently she had shared some of the deadly drug with Mary, and both women were small enough, frail enough, that the quantity was enough to kill them.

Moreover, the police had not measured the air quality during the raid, so there was no evidence that carbon monoxide had reached dangerous levels, though it likely would have with two hibachis. But one could argue, given their means of dying, that the women had lit the charcoal to stay warm. The only illegal act was Gladys giving Mary secobarbital. So CJ was completely off the hook and could pick up his van at any time.

"Tell me about Sarah Worthington again," the lawyer said.

"She was making a documentary about her mother," said CJ. "Including her death."

"The DA told me she's raising hell, demanding to be charged with murder."

CJ said, "That sounds like Sarah."

"You were going to narrate her film."

"Right."

"And how do you feel about it now?"

"I still agree with the principle, that all of us should be able to manage our own death, but I was not comfortable with the way Sarah was making a public statement about it. Her mother seemed to have dementia. I worried she actually didn't know what she was doing."

"That might be a case for murder," said Ann.

CJ nodded.

Charlie said, "I was under the impression the whole deal was Mary Worthington's idea. She didn't want to live as a blind artist."

"I guess this is all beside the point now," said Ann. "So, CJ, you can pick up your van at any time."

"I appreciate your help."

"I always wanted my last case to be an intriguing one. This will do. I've thought about this issue myself, especially now, given my circumstances. I would qualify for using the law. I'm leaning in that direction, but first I want to do some traveling."

"Anywhere in particular?" Charlie asked.

"Nothing too ambitious. I'll just take off and play it by ear."

"The professor did the same, more or less," said Charlie.

"Oh?"

94

After CJ summarized his travels, Ann said, "I'm jealous. Foot loose and fancy free."

CJ didn't feel foot loose and fancy free.

Charlie asked, "Did you find out how the police knew?"

"Gladys had told her sister, who didn't approve. She was the whistle-blower."

"The way things turned out, almost a blessing in disguise," said CJ.

"Yes, it was. And what kind of life have you had?" Ann asked Charlie.

"Since you brought it up, my life has gotten a little complicated lately and I could use some legal advice."

Charlie stopped to weigh her reaction.

"Go on," said Ann.

29

Molly decided to have a BBQ to celebrate the good news, which kept coming. On the day she'd driven CJ to Newport to pick up his van, they returned to find that Charlie's check had cleared. He had money in his pocket for the first time in six months. Taking Ann's advice, Charlie put most of it in a new checking account at a small bank. He moved into a motel, paying cash.

CJ, Charlie, Molly and Ann sat around a patio table in what felt to CJ like a going away or retirement party of some kind, the last occasion for all of them to be together. But Charlie had other ideas.

CJ was not terribly surprised by what followed because he had noticed a certain attraction between Charlie and Ann. At her office, when Charlie had picked her brain about his legal rights despite his daughter's power of attorney, rights that were considerable, CJ saw Ann falling under the spell of his former student's gift of gab. To a lawyer, and one wanting to rush into life in the time left to her, a charismatic writer like Charlie may have seemed like the very embodiment of a free spirit. They were the same age, sharing generational music that was foreign to CJ. They laughed a lot together.

Charlie said, "I have a proposition. It's going to sound crazy but hear me out. First let me ask everyone a question. When is the last time you saw the Milky Way?"

"I can't remember," said Molly.

Ann said, "God, it's been years. A summer vacation in Mexico. Maybe 10, 12 years ago."

"Professor?"

"More recently, in my travels. But I see your point. The first night I saw it, in the desert a few days after leaving Portland, I thought, What has happened to us, to create lives that hide this from us? Seeing the Milky Way changes your perspective on everything."

"Exactly. Eighty percent of Americans live where they can't see it. Eighty percent! And that number is growing. Even Beverly Beach had too much light pollution. So I say, to hell with statistics, let's all go where we can see it. Here's the deal. I'm going to Dallas to spend time with my brother. As good a place as any to figure out what to do about my daughter. Southern Utah is on the way, all that spiritual landscape in Monument Valley and the like. I know the professor digs it, especially the Goosenecks. So why not all go see it together? A couple weeks, a month. Camp a few days, get a motel to clean up. The trip would be good for our souls."

There was a silence.

Ann said, "You're serious?"

"Of course I'm serious. No one has any obligations to stay in Portland, right? We're all free spirits."

Molly said, "I would love to see that part of the country. CJ, you've talked so much about it. But do we have to camp?"

Charlie gave someone else a chance to respond before he said, "Not really."

CJ said, "It still gets pretty cold at night in the desert."

"I love the idea," said Ann. "And I'm with Molly, I like to shower every morning. When do we leave?"

"I'd say the sooner, the better," said Charlie. "Professor?"

"I'd have to think about it. I'm still processing stuff."

"Driving is great processing and brooding time," said Charlie. "I remember you saying that in class."

"And I can help with the driving," said Molly.

Everyone was waiting for CJ.

"This is an outrageous idea," said Ann. "Thank you for coming up with it."

"Stick with me, babe."

Laughter.

Molly said, "CJ, I think this would be good for you."

More waiting.

CJ said, "Sure, why not?"

Everyone except CJ applauded.

CJ Brooding
Multnomah Park Cemetery, Portland

CJ visited Helen's grave. All around him, from downtown to the westside hills, across the river to the sprawling eastside where the cemetery was, Portland was disrupted by growing pains, with construction projects and heavy traffic and detours, but here, surrounded by graves, CJ felt like he was in a relaxing landscape. He had brought flowers, something he'd not done in a long time, and a cup of coffee. He planned to linger a while.

Their marriage had been good, despite his later discovery of Helen's indiscretion with the woman in San Francisco, the physicist. He was glad she had never told him about her. Molly said Helen had wrestled with the idea but knew it would hurt him. Yes, it would have. But in Helen's silence he never saw a clue, and he didn't learn the truth until after she was gone.

The woman in San Francisco had not been a part of their ordeal with cancer. To CJ, this meant his own relationship was deeper than hers. More dependable. Through thick and thin, through good and bad, through joy and sorrow. He had made sure that Helen had not suffered or died alone. This meant something. Something profound.

Later, back in Molly's guest room, taking a break from reading, CJ went online to Amazon and typed in Charles Roberts. He was astounded by the number of books that appeared, over a dozen of them. Some had reviews, and a few were very favorable. CJ ordered a novel about a dying old man, a libretto that was described as "a tale of greed and mayhem during a gold rush in the Old West," and a novella because he was intrigued by the title, *A Writerly Revenge*. He selected expedited shipping to receive them before they hit the road.

Maybe the trip would be good for him. At least he enjoyed the company. Well, most of the time. Other times he wanted to be alone. But seeing Monument Valley and the Goosenecks of the San Juan River again justified any uncertainty he had. He was eager to get going.

30

CJ was napping when his cell phone rang. He found it and answered.

"Hello?"

"Can you believe this shit?"

"Sarah?"

"Listen, I need to know where you stand now. I'm trying to save my goddamn film here."

"I'm not sure what you mean."

"About your own decision, going to Monument Valley to do it and all that. I want to come along and film it. Are you okay with that?"

What the hell? She was coming at CJ with too many assumptions.

"Look, Sarah--"

"What? You've changed your mind?"

"I have cancer. I don't have to do anything."

"But that really doesn't speak to the issue, does it?"

CJ was silent.

"Well, does it?"

CJ thought a moment.

"To be honest, I don't know what I'm going to do."

"But you still might go to Utah to do it?"

"I might."

"If you do, can I film it?"

Jesus. CJ just wanted to be left alone.

"Look," he said, "I've been rethinking all of this. It didn't feel right at the beach. Your mother didn't seem to know what she was doing."

"What the fuck does that mean?"

"Sarah, I admire what you're trying to do, and I agree that everyone should be able to manage their own death but--"

"But you're too chickenshit to do anything about it."

"I'm not your enemy."

"Then why the fuck does it feel like you are?"

No one spoke for a moment.

"I'm sorry," said Sarah. "I just can't believe we went through all this and they're not pressing charges. I need to find another line of action for the film's ending."

CJ didn't respond.

"You have my number," said Sarah. "If you change your mind, give me a call."

"Good luck with--," he began but she already had hung up.

31

CJ received an email from Jan Smart. She wondered if everything was all right. They hadn't heard from him in a while.

CJ replied that everything was fine. However, he was not going to meet them in Mexico. He had some personal matters to take care of. He didn't explain, feeling a little guilty that he wasn't more straight forward with them. They had been good mentors and friends on the road.

Jan replied within an hour, Do you have a health issue? What's going on?

No, he sent back. I'm helping out a friend. Well, it wasn't totally untrue. He was helping Charlie.

You have a big heart, Jan returned.

She was giving him too much credit but CJ let it go at that.

He went back to reading. Charlie's books had arrived, and he was reading the shortest one, the libretto *Varmints*, which amounted to a story in verse. The setting was the Oregon gold rush in 1865, the story about a gold heist. But what intrigued CJ most was the revenge by Indians after ancestral bones are dug up by miners. Once again, as in the libretto he was writing while in CJ's class so many years ago, Charlie was telling a story from the Indian's point of view. Here was a sensibility they shared in common.

CJ's Reading

Gold is the measure of all things
Gold is the meaning of life
God said, Let there be light!
And the light was shining gold

Charles Roberts, *Varmints: A Libretto*

PART FOUR

O sweet spontaneous earth
E. E. Cummings

32

They left on a Monday under overcast skies in two cars. Charlie rode with CJ in his van. Ann decided to drive and then take Charlie to Dallas after seeing Monument Valley, and Molly rode with her.

The forecast along their route was for several days of intermittent rain. Before they departed, CJ had raised the issue of how many miles they would drive in a day, given his bad back. Charlie suggested that Molly could drive and CJ could crash on the van's bed when he got uncomfortable. A compromise of three hundred miles became their daily goal. Most of the trip would be on the Interstate.

They were out of Portland but not yet to Hood River when Charlie said, "Are you all right? I get the vibe something is bothering you."

CJ looked at him. But he didn't reply.

Charlie said, "I'm sorry. It's none of my business."

CJ said, "I have prostate cancer. But it's no big deal. I'm okay with it."

"What, it's in remission?"

"No."

"You're doing treatment?"

"No."

"So you're prepared to accept the consequences?"

CJ said, "That's a fancy way to ask if I'm ready to die. The answer is yes. The fact is, I was ready before I knew I had cancer. I'd made plans for death by hibachi in Monument Valley."

"Holy ..." Charlie began but didn't finish.

CJ said, "I came to Portland to say goodbye to Matt. I'd been having stomach pains and went to the VA. That's when they found the cancer. Then I learned about Sarah's film, and you know the rest."

"I didn't realize you've been through so much shit."

"Matt dying is the worst," said CJ.

"So where are you with all this now?"

"Good question. The cancer makes the situation less urgent. What's bothered me is losing the ability to make my own decisions. I will not become a vegetable, and I won't go

105

through the treatment nightmare that my wife went through. So where does that leave me? With death by hibachi. I mean, it's the best alternative. But if I wait too long, a stroke could take away my independence. I don't want to die but it's better to go too early than to risk a stroke. So I'd decided to light the charcoal at Monument Valley but say goodbye to Matt first."

"Man," said Charlie.

They drove a while in silence.

Charlie asked, "Does Molly know this?"

"About the cancer. Not the other. This is just between us."

"Of course."

"Without treatment, I have a couple years. I'm still deciding whether I want them or not."

Charlie nodded.

"How about some music?" said CJ and turned on the van's CD player.

Get out of town, sang Chris Connor.

33

They spent their first night in Joseph near Wallowa Lake. CJ was ready to call it quits at a rest stop near La Grande but Charlie convinced him to continue another seventy miles because Joseph was one of Charlie's old stomping grounds. He wanted to show it to Ann.

But Joseph had changed since the 1980s. Charlie had written most of the libretto for *Dark Mission* in a cabin on the lake, he said, offered gratis by the academic parents of a friend. Despite having few credits as a writer, he felt treated with respect by them by the mere fact that he was working on something many hours a day, a writer who wasn't talking but *writing*. Charlie hung out at a local tavern and became accepted by the regulars, most of whom had never met an actual working writer before. In Joseph at the time, the arts were exotic.

Now Joseph had the aura of a tourist trap. Galleries and boutiques were everywhere, catering to the summer vacation masses who had discovered the town as a gateway to the lake. Charlie found the scene depressing and wanted to leave, backtracking to get a motel in nearby Enterprise, but Molly and Ann wanted to browse the galleries and boutiques, and CJ wanted to stop moving. They got a motel in town.

CJ Brooding
Bald Eagle Motel, Joseph

It wasn't Charlie's snoring that kept CJ awake, it was his own mind. He kept thinking about his own connection to Joseph. The memorial grave of Old Chief Joseph was just out of town, and the unsuccessful flight of the Nez Perce to Canada, led by the son, young Chief Joseph, had been the subject of CJ's first book, based on his doctoral dissertation, *From Where the Sun Now Stands.*

Before the flight, the traditional grave of Old Chief Joseph had been desecrated and its skull removed as a souvenir. The present memorial, with its spectacular view of Wallowa Lake and mountains, had been built as a WPA project. Young Joseph, who died decades later, was buried on the reservation in Washington.

The image of old Joseph's skull displayed on a stick and paraded for cheering soldiers and white civilians had come to CJ early in his research. This may or may not have happened. Maybe the skull became a paper weight on a desk. But CJ pictured the extreme as a kind of poster for his thesis, not widely accepted by historians of his generation, that the government's American Indian policy amounted to genocide. Most historians preferred the term assimilation.

CJ had studied America at its worst because he believed a nation that did not look in the mirror at its worst deeds had no hope of redemption and progress toward "life, liberty and the pursuit of happiness" for all its citizens. "If men were angels," Hamilton had written, "no government would be necessary." But men were anything but.

Through his career, CJ had believed in the possibility of America, that its institutions defined a government that could bend to give everyone a better life. Admit your sins to move beyond them, was the history professor's message to America.

In retirement, CJ fretted that he had made a mistake. Historians had barely scratched the surface of America's misdeeds. Now, with the advent of social media, with the ascension of Donald Trump, a deep deformity had surfaced, the unrequited racism of masses of angry and frustrated citizens eager for revenge and a return to simpler times. Simple because their racism was more hidden.

Helen scoffed at her husband's cynicism when she was alive. She told CJ he was over-playing his hand, that genuine progress had been made and would continue to be made, in race relations, in gender relations, in all areas of social and political life, small steps to be sure but progress nonetheless. She never got CJ to change his mind but her faith rubbed off a little and now and again he admitted the possibility she might be right.

34

They reached Boise in the middle of the next afternoon, and CJ wanted to stop. He wanted to hang around the Basque district.

The sky was overcast, threatening rain.

"Not the best weather for exploring," said Charlie. "Maybe we should go on for another hour or two."

"I'd like to see the Basque district," said Ann.

"Me, too," said Molly.

CJ gave Charlie a look that read, *You're outnumbered.*

As on the previous night, they rented two motel rooms, men together and women together. They cleaned up and ventured out for sight-seeing and dinner. The threatening rain never started.

That evening, after walking through the several blocks of Basque restaurants and shops and after visiting a museum, they chose a cafe to dine.

As they relaxed over after-dinner drinks, CJ got everyone's attention.

"I have something important to say," he said. "Charlie, you already know all this."

He sipped his beer.

"All of you know I have prostate cancer. I think everyone knows that I'm skipping treatment. I see no need to extend my life. I've had a very blessed life, as a matter of fact. But the way the world is, and without a family around me, and at my age, I see no reason to ask doctors to try and extend my life.

"On the contrary, I'd rather engage their help to end it." He thought he heard a quick gasp from Molly. "Before I was diagnosed, I'd decided to take my life in Monument Valley. Death by hibachi, just like Mary Worthington. How weird to meet her, let me tell you! I wasn't depressed, just angry that I had to do this alone. I've had a great life! Now I wanted a great death, and I wanted medical help to do that. But I don't qualify because I don't have a terminal disease. Well, guess what? Life is a terminal disease. Try telling that to a doctor."

"Please stop," Molly suddenly said.

She got up from the table and hurried off. Ann got up to follow her.

"I'll calm her down," said Ann.

When she was gone, CJ said, "Guess I should have kept my mouth shut."

The women never returned. When they got back to the motel, Charlie knocked on their door.

CJ was sitting on the bed when Charlie returned.

"She's fine," Charlie said.

"Good," said CJ.

"I hope we can make Salt Lake City tomorrow. A little over three hundred."

"We'll see."

35

CJ woke up while Charlie was still snoring. The sun was coming up. He dressed and went to the adjacent all-night cafe.

He found Molly sitting alone in a booth. He hesitated, not sure whether she wanted company. Then she motioned for him to join her.

"You could've told me," she said right off.

"I knew how upset you'd be."

"That's no excuse. Close friends shouldn't keep secrets from one another."

"I apologize."

"Of course I disagree with you."

"I know. We shouldn't talk about it."

Molly nodded as the waitress arrived.

But Molly did want to talk about it. At breakfast with the others she suggested a change for variety, she'd ride with CJ and Charlie with Ann. CJ wondered what she was up to.

He found out as soon as they were back on the Interstate.

"Don't you believe in God?" Molly asked.

Oh boy. CJ collected his thoughts.

"I believe in Nature," he finally said.

"Well, who created Nature? God did."

"Molly, these are timeless and complicated questions."

"Look, Mr. Smarty Pants, you may have read many more books than I have but if all books do is make you stop believing in God, what good are they?"

Again he asked himself how far to go with this.

He said, "There's a very old argument by Bertrand Russell. He's a philosopher."

"I know who he is," Molly snapped.

"If everything needs a First Cause, then God needs a First Cause. If something can exist without a First Cause, then it might as well be the universe as God."

CJ wondered if Molly was letting this sink in or just was quiet.

She said, "Are you going to do it there?"

"Do what where?"

"Kill yourself in Monument Valley."

"Certainly not in the presence of others."

"CJ!"

"No, I'm not going to do it when we get there."

"You don't sound very convincing."

She was right. He hadn't even convinced himself.

36

That night they got to see the Milky Way. The gray skies overseeing their trip early on broke up in late afternoon. They stopped for the day at a motel just north of Salt Lake City.

After dinner, Charlie proposed driving out of town to see what kind of night sky they could see. The Milky Way wouldn't be visible until around midnight, he'd learned on the Internet, but the night would be moonless and he was game if they rest were. Let's do it, they all agreed, though CJ was skeptical they'd see much.

They took Ann's car. After driving a few miles off a service road into the brush, Ann pulled over and stopped. They all piled out.

Charlie was the first to identify it.

"Ladies and gentlemen, the Milky Way!" he proclaimed, pointing to the eastern horizon. He embraced Ann, grinning.

CJ found it disappointing, but the smudge of light rising in the east was indeed the Milky Way.

He said, "It's going to be much brighter and mind-boggling at Monument Valley, believe me."

Molly said, "I think it's mind-boggling right now. How can anyone look at this and not believe in God?"

CJ figured the remark was meant for him but he didn't take the bait, if that's what it was.

Charlie said, "I agree with you. Of course, God means many things to many people. To me God means the natural universe, the amazing wide spectrum of life we are born into."

"What about Jesus Christ?" Molly asked.

"What about him?" Charlie replied.

"Do you believe in him?"

"Absolutely. He was the far-out hippy guru of his day."

"He's the son of God," said Molly.

Ann said, "I'm Jewish."

CJ almost laughed. Leave it to religion to present a conversational quagmire.

"And I'm a Scorpio!" said Charlie. "Sex and death, so watch out!"

He embraced Ann again and twirled her around.

They turned quiet, looking at the Milky Way.

"The longer you look at it," said Ann, "the more overwhelming it is."

"And like the professor says, you ain't seen nothing yet."

"A shooting star!" Ann said.

"I missed it," said CJ.

They scanned the skies until another meteor streaked between the stars. Everyone had seen it.

Ann said, "I hope we're not getting an early start tomorrow."

"No way," said Charlie.

They looked at the Milky Way, and everyone was silent.

It was almost noon before they were back on the Interstate, men and women riding together again. They had a modest goal, Moab, not much over two hundred miles from Salt Lake City.

At breakfast Charlie said he had something he wanted to share with everyone. He took a folded paper out of his wallet.

"I did a terrible job of explaining my sense of God last night," he said. "As it happens, there's a passage in one of my favorite books that does it much better. I've been carrying this around for a long time."

He unfolded the paper and began to read:

"Here I must confess that I know nothing whatever about true underlying reality, having never met any. There are many people who say they have, I know, but they've been luckier than I. For my own part I am pleased enough with surfaces – in fact they alone seem to me to be of much importance. Such things for example as the grasp of a child's hand in your own, the flavor of an apple, the embrace of friend or lover, the silk of a girl's thigh, the sunlight on rock and leaves, the feel of music, the bark of a tree, the abrasion of granite and sand, the plunge of clear water into a pool, the face of the wind – what else is there? What else do we need?"

He folded the paper and returned it to his wallet.

"That's so beautiful.. Who wrote it?" Ann asked.

"It's from *Desert Solitaire* by Edward Abbey. It's about his experiences as a park ranger in southern Utah."

"I'd like to read it," Ann said.

"Know it, professor?"

"By reputation," said CJ.

Charlie smiled at Molly but she gave no indication if the passage had clarified anything for her.

CJ, sensing potential conflict, said, "We'd better get going."

Back on the road after a late lunch, Charlie said, "I'd like to run something by you."

"Okay," said CJ.

"What if I ride with Ann and Molly rides with you? It's no big deal, if that would make you uncomfortable."

"Maybe it is a big deal." CJ smiled.

"I think she's really something. Leave it to me to be attracted to a woman with only a short time to live."

"Go for it. But I don't think Molly will ride with me."

"Thanks, professor."

The landscape was changing south of Salt Lake City, distant snow-capped mountains giving way to the rolling hills of high desert, then to a flatter browner brush-filled groundscape and the occasional appearance of sandstone formations, gradual at first, like odd splotches of rust color thrown down for contrast, but which would change dramatically to high mounds and red cliffs as they got closer to Moab.

"I read your novel about the writer," said CJ.

It was the story of an unpublished novelist who gets a flattering letter from an agent, only later to discover the very same boilerplate letter was received by many of his colleagues. The agent is a scam artist, which outrages the writer enough to take creative and outrageous revenge.

"A Writerly Revenge?"

"Right. I enjoyed it. How much of it is autobiographical?"

Charlie laughed.

"The inevitable question. I never know what to say. None of it, and all of it. Depends on how you mean."

"I'll be reading more of your work."

Would he be? He shouldn't have said so. CJ already was thinking about lighting the charcoal in Monument Valley after all, if he could figure out how to separate himself from the others. One thing he had learned was that an intentional rational suicide should not be a public event.

CJ's Reading

The serious writer's only job is to write. It's not to appear on television. It's not to butt-hole the marketplace. It's not to write what the public wants. It's to write what he needs to write, what he cannot not write. A writer writes for the gods. A writer writes for posterity. Thus it's a lonely job – interrupted only occasionally by the strike of lightning, the sudden appearance of an engaged reader ...

Charles Roberts, *A Writerly Revenge*

39

The Milky Way! After getting a motel in Moab, Charlie suggested they crash early. He then woke everyone at 2 a.m. They all took the van, Molly making no objection, and CJ didn't have to drive far out of town for the dark night to wrap them in wonder, which was articulated by Ann.

"I'd forgotten how dark it can get at night!"

CJ pulled to the side of the road. They all got out. In the darkness was an early morning chill.

"My God," said Molly.

This is more like it, thought CJ. The stars above were overwhelming in number, pinpoints of light everywhere you looked, in varying configurations and densities, like an infestation of tiny insects of light, and in the east, higher than last night, the Milky Way like an incandescent haze of smoke. CJ had seen this many times in his travels but the sight always filled him with awe and humility.

Charlie said, "Pity this busy monster manunkind, not. ... listen: there's a hell of a good universe next door, let's go."

"What's that?" Ann asked.

"From Cummings. Part of a poem."

"Do you know more?"

"Not the whole thing. But there's also this: a world of made is not a world of born – pity poor flesh and trees, poor stars and stones, but never this fine specimen of hypermagical ultraomnipotence."

CJ repeated, "Hypermagical ultraomnipotence. Perfect."

Ann said, "Wow."

"My favorite poet," said Charlie.

"There!" said Molly, as a bright shooting star streaked overhead. And shortly another.

CJ said, "I wonder if there's a shower tonight."

"No idea," said Charlie.

After a silence, as they all looked upward, Ann said, "We should have brought blankets so we could watch lying down."

"Good idea," said Charlie. "Next time."

They remained outside in the chill, standing, looking skyward. After a while Ann said, "My neck is getting stiff."

"We'll bring blankets tomorrow," said Charlie.

"And sweaters," said Molly.

After a while CJ said, "Shall we?" and they climbed back into the van.

CJ Brooding
Red Rock Motel, Moab

Should he or shouldn't he?

Moab was the gateway to the canyonlands that, more than any other landscape in America, moved CJ into a quiet, spiritual place in which he felt, in ways he could not explain, insignificant and connected at the same time. Somehow he was a part of this grandeur of red sandstone and rock, of towers and spires and stone bridges and cliffs, if only by his ability to stand in awe before it, to let its magnificence absorb him like a rain drop falling into the ocean, making him feel insignificant but also inseparable. He belonged here, and this is where he wanted to die.

But was it time? His ace in the hole, cancer, had removed urgency and promised death soon enough; he would not end up a vegetable kept alive by the well-meaning life-affirming obsession of doctors. Unless, of course, the doctor at the VA was wrong in his diagnosis. What if he actually didn't have cancer? Why in hell hadn't he gotten a second opinion?

He hated the lack of discipline in his mind, this bombardment of questions, the loss of an external order that Helen always had brought to his dilemmas. Why not just go back to his original plan and be done with it? After all, there were no great demands on him to keep living, no family, no legacy. No family. No legacy.

He made a decision and left Charlie snoring in the motel. Starbucks was opening, where he could use their wifi to send an email.

Sarah, he typed on the Kindle Fire keyboard, *I am in Moab. I am going back to my original plan, and I would like you to film it. I'm staying at the Red Rock Motel. How soon can you get here?*

He sent the email. If she left right away, with mostly an Interstate highway to drive, she should be able to get to Moab in three days. That would give him time to figure out how to handle Molly.

40

In the morning Charlie proposed their tour for the day. He'd been researching the area on the Internet and had downloaded maps and pictures to his phone, which he showed everyone.

Moab was perfectly located, very close to two national parks, Arches and Canyonlands, and a smaller state park Dead Horse Point. Monument Valley and Goosenecks were only one-hundred-fifty miles south. There was so much to see.

"I suggest a day for Arches," said Charlie, "and the next for Dead Horse Point and Canyonlands, which are next to each other. Then the following day head south."

Nobody had any objections.

"I'd like to do Arches in two cars," said CJ. "I have something personal I want to talk about with Molly."

Molly looked at him with concern.

"Then you'll ride with me," Ann said to Charlie, and they embraced.

CJ said, "Let's meet here for lunch at one. Does that work?"

Again, nobody objected.

After Charlie and Ann were gone, Molly said, "I don't like the feel of this."

"After we see the sights here for a few days, I'm getting you a flight back to Portland. I'm not returning."

She seemed to be waiting for more. CJ had considered how much he should tell her. As little as possible, was his first thought.

He said, "Portland has too many ghosts."

"I think you're lying. I think you plan to go through with that BBQ thing."

That BBQ thing!

Molly went on.

"We've been friends for a long time, CJ. I was best friends with Helen. I know how hard it's been for you without her. But this is no reason to lie to me."

She waited.

Finally CJ lied, "I don't know what I'm going to do, except stay away from Portland."

"Please don't do this. Talk to a counselor. They have professionals who know how to deal with depression in old age and the rest."

"For Christ's sake, Molly, I'm not depressed! As a matter of fact, I feel like I have a new purpose. I know what I'm doing."

"The BBQ thing?"

He hated the way that sounded. But he wasn't going to defend himself. He didn't have to.

CJ said, "We're in the most spiritual landscape in America. Let's enjoy it. Let's go see the Arches."

Molly got up from the table.

"What you are going to do is a sin, CJ."

She turned and walked out of the cafe.

CJ sat and sipped his coffee. When the waitress came by, he refused a refill and asked for the check. He had no desire to tour the Arches alone. Instead he decided to drive to the airport and get Molly her ticket back to Portland.

41

CJ was late for lunch. He'd returned to the motel after buying Molly's ticket and fell asleep. He found Charlie and Ann at a corner table.

"I thought Molly would be with you," said Charlie.

CJ told them everything. They could handle it.

"This is so against her religion," said Ann.

CJ said, "I didn't tell her. She guessed it."

"I'm going to go see how she is."

Ann stood up, gave Charlie a squeeze on the shoulder, and left.

Right away Charlie said, "I'm disappointed in you."

The remark took CJ by surprise.

"I thought we were on the same page about this."

"About managing your own death, of course. But not with the flip of a coin. Mary Worthington was an artist who was going blind. Robin Williams had early dementia that was destroying his quick wit. Living circumstances were changing radically for them, soon it would be impossible to be who they are. It's perfectly understandable that they would object. Their deaths were existential statements of personal identification. But what are your circumstances? You hate Trump? You're depressed by climate change? You have early prostate cancer? Well, boo hoo. Give me a break."

CJ glanced around, for fear someone was listening. A confrontation with Charlie was the last thing he expected.

CJ said, "You don't know the whole story."

"I sure as hell hope not. Because you act like a man wearing blinders. You talk about the Milky Way providing perspective. Well, bring some of that perspective to the news that upsets you so much. There's a hell of a lot of amazing stories out there, inspirational stories, even if the media doesn't give them the attention they deserve. There are doctors in Syria, volunteering from all over the world, who keep working even when their hospitals are bombed and bombed again. There are volunteers in Haiti and Puerto Rico who are still helping storm victims long after the government gave up. Somewhere, at this very moment, some stranger is rescuing someone from a burning house, a burning car, or delivering a stranger's baby on the floor of a supermarket. Jesus Christ, professor, the country is full of mind-boggling wondrous acts by anonymous nobodies. Unsung heroes are everywhere."

Charlie stopped, exhausted.

CJ said, "I appreciate what you're saying. And I plead guilty, I don't focus enough on the good people in this world. But this has nothing to do with what I'm going to do."

Charlie had no response.

"I contacted Sarah," said CJ. "She'll be here in a few days to film everything."

Charlie nodded.

"Okay. And ...?"

"And what?"

"How does that change things?"

"It gives me something I haven't had for a long time. Purpose. Legacy."

"You don't think you have a legacy?"

"I don't."

"Because you don't have children? That's ridiculous. You're a teacher. You've touched a hundred minds. You've touched mine."

"I actually understand that," said CJ. "Somehow it hasn't felt like it's enough."

"I'm a writer with almost no audience," Charlie said. "I know about legacies, believe me. You have to keep the faith that you haven't been wasting your time. All you have to do is touch one person out there, and your purpose is validated. Just one. Legacy isn't a popularity contest."

"Being in Sarah's film feels like my legacy."

After a moment, Charlie said, "That actually makes sense to me. I think you're wrong about teaching, you have a greater legacy than you realize, but if you don't feel it, you don't feel it. I can see how letting her film you, being the star of the film, really, would give you a sense of purpose."

"Do I still disappoint you?"

Charlie grinned.

"I exaggerated a little before. You were my favorite teacher, don't you know that?"

"I didn't. Why was that?"

"You didn't tell me to shut up as often as the others."

CJ Brooding
Red Rock Motel, Moab

He wished he could die outside under the stars. Of course, that would mean changing his method, which he was not about to do. Death by hibachi, and this method alone, offered the tranquil passing that CJ wanted. He would go to sleep and never wake up.

He recalled something an astronaut had said about seeing Earth from space, how it put human life in a new perspective. CJ felt something similar under the night sky, something spiritual.

This spiritual experience belonged to American Indians nightly, if the skies were clear, as natural a phenomenon as the sun rising. The United States, with its policies of expansion and greed, with its policies of genocide, had done more than destroy a people's culture, it had destroyed the mirror of the night sky, a canopy of learning available to anyone, where human smallness was indisputable; it had removed the most direct experience available to the species to put its purpose in perspective. Eighty percent of Americans no longer could see the Milky Way from where they lived. Eighty percent were made blind to reality.

As an historian CJ well knew that no Indian tribe had created a perfect society, that it was easy to romanticize Indian lifestyles. But some things they had done right. They had not become addicted to growth. They had not been driven by greed and ownership.

He remembered a Cayuse curse on the white man:

Only after the last tree has been cut down. Only after the last river has been poisoned. Only after the last fish has been caught. Only then will you learn that money cannot be eaten.

42

CJ woke up to find Charlie excitedly talking on the phone. The motel drapes were open, but the lunchtime sunlight was covered by an afternoon gray sky.

"We definitely will see it tomorrow," Charlie was saying. "See you at dinner."

He hung up and saw CJ sitting on the edge of the bed.

"Who were you talking to?" CJ asked.

"Ann. I had to tell her what I discovered. You'll never guess what's in Dead Horse Point State Park. The cliff where Thelma and Louise drove into history. Can you believe it?"

CJ stood up and stretched.

Charlie said, "We should check it out tomorrow."

"Sounds good."

It was too early for dinner. Each decided to pass time by reading.

The thunder started suddenly. A fast-moving storm was passing overhead, flashes of lightning reflected off the window panes, and at one point their reading lamps flickered on and off.

Charlie stepped to the window.

"Check out this hail!"

Ice the size of golf balls pounded the parking lot. People caught outside ran for cover.

The telephone rang.

Charlie answered, "Hello? ... It's incredible. ... I could eat. ... No way. You should stay inside, too. One of those things on the noggin could knock you out. ... Okay. Bye."

He hung up.

"Ann wanted to go walking in it. I set her straight."

"Good."

The hail continued for several minutes. The thunder and lightning moved farther off and then stopped. The entire storm had lasted less than ten minutes, leaving behind a drizzle of rain.

"I love thunderstorms," said CJ. "They're a good reminder that Nature wins."

"Nature wins," Charlie repeated.

The phone rang again.

Charlie said, "I bet the ladies are ready for dinner."
He was right.

43

It was still raining the next morning. At breakfast they agreed to abandon the ambitious tour of two parks and instead just find the cliff at Dead Horse Point that Thelma and Louise had driven off of. To ease tensions between himself and Molly, CJ suggested they go in two cars, women and men together as before.

Ann led the way, following a map Charlie had sent to her phone. They drove southwest on the highway to a service road, then turned to continue almost twenty miles into the isolated terrain. Occasionally the dirt road would dip to cross a dry river bed, rise and continue before dipping again. They saw no other cars along the way.

If she hadn't been paying attention, Ann could have driven off the cliff herself. It was unguarded and unmarked. Seeing her approach it without slowing down, CJ beeped the van horn to alert her. The two vehicles stopped, and everyone got out. The rain had stopped.

"Oh my God," said Ann, seeing the view of the Colorado Basin below, a long stretch of river and canyons, as spectacular as the Grand Canyon.

CJ said, "How do we know this is the place?"

Charlie brought up a map on his phone.

"It's where the park map says it is. I'll double check." He brought up a photograph. "Here is the scene at the end of the movie. What do you think? Looks like the same place to me."

He passed around the phone.

Ann said, "There should be a plaque or something. That ending has become iconic."

"Of what?" Molly asked.

It was the first time she'd spoken all morning.

"Of feminine power," said Ann. "A woman's ability to control her own destiny, on her own terms."

Molly looked dubious and moved away. She stopped and stared out at the view, looking very much alone.

"You hear that?" CJ said.

He'd heard distant thunder. He scanned the horizon all around him.

"Now that looks menacing," CJ said, pointing to a billow of dark clouds to the southwest.

"Think it's coming our way?" Charlie asked.

"I have no idea, but I don't think it's a good idea to wait and find out."

"It looks pretty far away," said Ann.

There was more thunder.

Ann said, "Is it sexist that there's no plaque here?"

"I think you're exaggerating the importance of the movie and its ending," said CJ.

"Maybe. What do you think?" Ann asked Charlie.

Before he had a chance to answer, it started raining again, this time harder than before. The heavens had turned on a spigot full blast without warning.

They all raced into the vehicles. Suddenly there was thunder louder than before.

"Where the hell did this come from?" said Charlie.

"Time to get back," said CJ.

He beeped the horn at Ann. She got the message and started off.

As they drove, the storm intensified at an alarming rate. Pools began to collect on the impervious dry ground. The first river bed they crossed now had a stream of water flowing along it. The next one, more water still. And the third looked like a small creek.

Ann stopped.

"She's afraid to cross," said Charlie. He opened the van door.

"What are you doing?" asked CJ.

"I'm going to drive her across."

"Is it safe?"

"It better be. We can't sit around here. The brunt of the storm hasn't even hit yet."

Charlie raced in the heavy rain to the car and got in behind the wheel. Through an open window, he waved at CJ and moved Ann's car forward.

As far as CJ could tell, he made it through the water without difficulty. Charlie stopped to wait for CJ to follow him.

Suddenly a strong wind rocked the van. What was going on? CJ moved the van slowly forward toward the creek bed and into the water.

Hearing a sound, CJ turned and saw the torrent of water and debris just before it crashed against the van, rocking it. Charlie was out of the car and yelling something at him, waving his arms, but CJ was concentrating on getting out of the van, which rocked as if it were about to turn over. He pushed the door open and put one leg into the churning water, then lost his balance and fell. As he struggled to keep his head above water, a log hit his head, then another, and CJ lost consciousness. He was oblivious to the cries and shouts that followed his body as it was swept away by the flash flood.

44

No one could find CJ's body. After two days, Molly used her ticket to fly home, and Charlie and Ann continued on to Dallas.

Sarah had learned on the news about the storms in southern Utah. When she received no reply from CJ to her emails or voice mail messages, she became concerned.

On the day Sarah arrived in Moab, hikers found CJ's body miles away from where he had been swept up by the flood. At the Red Rock Motel, the clerk told Sarah what had happened.

On the evening news in her motel room, Sarah learned that a body had been found and was believed to be the missing old man but actually had yet to be identified. They still were looking for someone who could identify the body.

She contacted the police first thing in the morning. She'd considered what approach to take, deciding to identify herself as CJ's niece. Uncle Carlton was her favorite uncle.

To her surprise, they took her to see the body immediately. She wasn't vetted in any way.

When the mortician pulled down the sheet, Sarah gasped. It was CJ, yes, but a grotesque version of him, ashen-pale in color, body looking deflated, skin splotched, a distorted scowl on the lips of an open mouth. She said yes, that's him, and quickly turned away. She thought she might get sick.

Sarah was so disturbed by the sight of the body that she almost blew it. She almost left then and there. But before she was escorted from the room, she stopped and asked a favor.

"May I have a moment with him alone, to pay my respects?"

The mortician said, "Certainly."

He brought out the body again and left.

When she was alone, Sarah pulled down the sheet, avoiding a glance at the face. She brought out a small video camera from her purse. She bent over the body and in the viewfinder brought CJ's face close and into focus, struggling to maintain a professional distance, then started recording. She shot video for several minutes.

She put away the camera. She pulled the sheet back over the body.

"Rest in peace, CJ," she said softly. Her voice had cracked.

In the parking lot, Sarah gathered her thoughts. This new footage should be enough to rescue the ending of her film. The look on CJ's face still haunted her. Maybe she could present it in such a way that it would haunt the American public as well. Maybe it would start people talking about the personal management of death.

Sarah still needed narration. If she couldn't find someone, she'd do it herself. She'd start writing narration tonight.

Sarah started the engine.

END

ABOUT THE AUTHOR

Last Rights is Charles Deemer's seventh book for Round Bend Press. He is retired and a three-time finalist for the Oregon Book Award (Drama). He lives in Milwaukie, Oregon, with his wife, Harriet.

More information is available at
http://www.ibiblio.org/cdeemer/bio.htm

Contact: cdeemer@yahoo.com